THEY CAME TO THE MOJAVE

Grant Whitman—A crack Army intelligence man, he was risking his life undercover to try to track down the Mexican bandit chief who was running wild on both sides of the border.

Eustacia Kibbe—Raised by a cavalry sergeant, she would not quit on her difficult marriage, scraping to make ends meet and to hold on to her children. Now she made the dangerous trip to search for her wandering husband—but was it out of love or duty?

Francisco Arango—The sun-baked, blood-thirsty desert rat who drew strength from the brutal Mojave and ravaged the outlying ranches as he pleased.

Philip Kibbe—Dreamer and would-be adventurer, he got swept up by the power of Arango and now is the main gun-runner for the very outlaw who might destroy his family.

The Stagecoach Series
Ask your bookseller for the books you have missed

STAGECOACH STATION 16:
MOJAVE

Hank Mitchum

 Created by the producers of
Wagons West, White Indian,
and Saga of the Southwest.

Chairman of the Board: Lyle Kenyon Engel

BANTAM BOOKS
TORONTO • NEW YORK • LONDON • SYDNEY • AUCKLAND

STAGECOACH STATION 16: MOJAVE

*A Bantam Book / published by arrangement with
Book Creations, Inc.*

Bantam edition / February 1985

*Produced by Book Creations, Inc.
Chairman of the Board: Lyle Kenyon Engel.*

ISBN 0-553-24662-3

Published simultaneously in the United States and Canada

STAGECOACH STATION 16:

MOJAVE

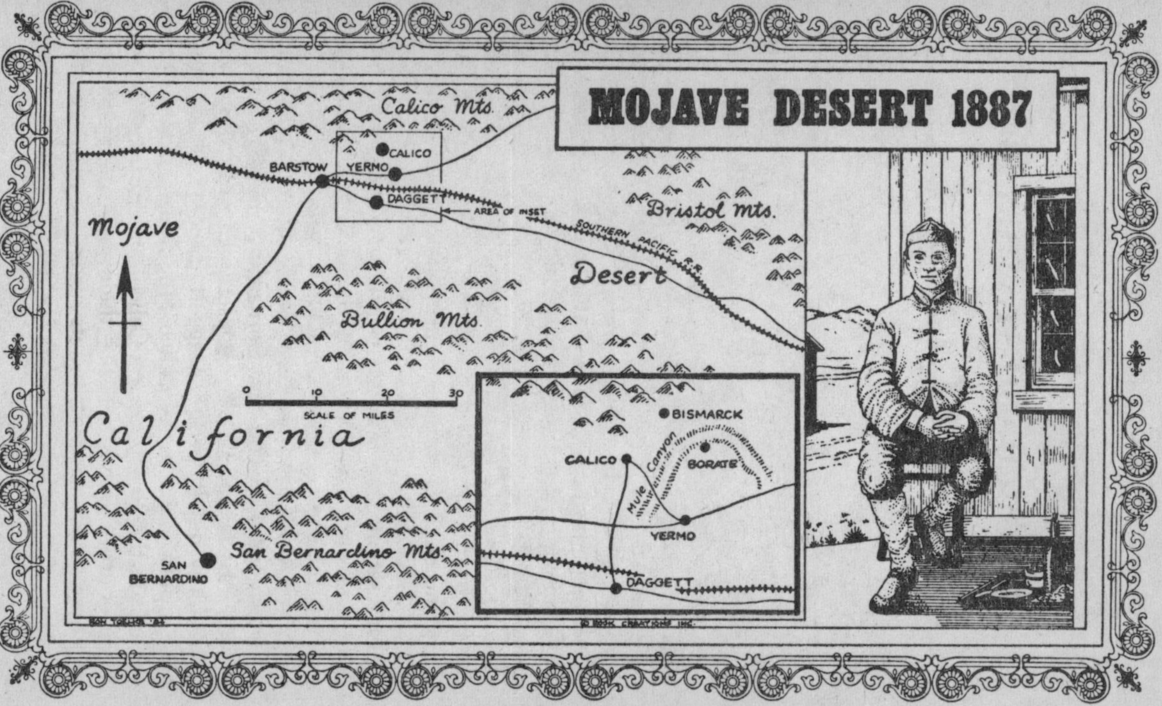
MOJAVE DESERT 1887
Calico Mts.
CALICO
YERMO
BARSTOW
DAGGETT
AREA OF INSET
Bristol mts.
SOUTHERN PACIFIC R.R.
Mojave
Desert
Bullion Mts.
0
10
20
30
SCALE OF MILES
California
San Bernardino Mts.
SAN BERNARDINO
BISMARCK
CALICO
Mule Canyon
BORATE
YERMO
DAGGETT

Chapter One

Eustacia Kibbe, dressed as a young man, sat on the Concord stage box between the driver and the express messenger. On this late afternoon in September 1887, it seemed the heavily loaded stagecoach was the only thing moving across California's Mojave Desert. There were fifteen other passengers, nine inside and six on the roof behind Eustacia. All rough miners, their shoulders, knees, and scuff-booted feet knocked together with the sway of the stage and the team's mile-eating gait. They were too tired to notice anything anymore. Conversations had long ago ceased, the dreams of rich mines slowly ground down by the passing bleak white desert, the scrub grass and cactus.

The Concord stage, one of an independent line, had originated out of San Bernardino, and by way of Cajon Pass and the Mojave Desert, it was rolling away the ninety miles north to Daggett. Daggett was a mining supply town in the Calico Mountains, feeding the miners in the silver camp of Calico, an additional seven miles north, and processing their raw ore. The San Bernardino coach would end its run in Daggett, and the

Calico Stage Line would carry ongoing passengers into the silver camp.

Eustacia Kibbe wondered if the Calico stage would be as dilapidated as this one. Then she decided that there was nothing really wrong with this coach. It was certainly in good mechanical order. It was the Mojave Desert that had made it seem old. The black leather of the front and rear boots was cracked from the sun and heat. The bright red of its body was faded to a washed-out watermelon color. The low iron railing, fencing in the driver's box and ringing the top, was flaky with rust in spots—courtesy of sudden, torrential desert storms. But the stage rocked with the same old cradling sureness. The two thoroughbraces, three-inch-thick leather straps on which the body of the coach was slung, were as supple and sound as ever and were still capable of absorbing the worst of the Mojave's punishment. The stage performed the same as the day it had been built, but the Mojave Desert had aged it beyond its years.

In a way, Eustacia reasoned, the Mojave had done the same to her. When she had undertaken this journey to Calico, she had decided that dressing in men's pants, shirt, mackinaw, and slouch hat would minimize the desert hardships. She had never dreamed that people would really take her for a young man, but they had, one and all, including the driver and the express messenger, Frank Eberson. Immediately seeing the benefits of this, especially in the current rough company, Eustacia had allowed the disguise to continue, speaking little, in fear her voice might give her away. She became "the quiet young man." Now, as she glanced at the men sitting behind her, she thought it hardly mattered. Everyone was so tired, she doubted they would recognize their own mothers.

Underneath her rough clothes, however, was a wholly different person. Eustacia was a thirty-one-year-

2

old woman of medium height and slender build. Her hair was wheat colored and cut fairly short. Her large brown eyes were slanted slightly downward at the corners, with hooding lids. They made her look sleepy or, as her husband, Philip, had often said, sensuous.

The thought of Philip brought back the thought of why she was sitting on this stage box at all. Some six months earlier, Philip had left San Bernardino for Calico, hoping to establish a silver claim. She hadn't heard from him since, and now Eustacia was on her way to find Philip—or so she fervently wished.

The reason Eustacia presumed she could do this was what made her different from many other women. Her background had been more hard honed than most. Her father had been an army sergeant. When Eustacia as a little girl had lost her mother on the Arizona frontier, her father had transferred to Fort Mojave—one hundred twenty miles due east of Calico—determined to raise his own child. He had not reared Eustacia as a boy, but he had made sure she could ride, drive a team, and shoot, three skills that would insure her survival on the Mojave.

Eustacia was as well educated as most of her contemporaries, and she was practical, a carryover from army life. Sixteen years of marriage had also instilled a survival instinct, a toughness. However, she always knew that down deep lay the remnants of a fifteen-year-old romantic. It had certainly surfaced when she had named her two daughters—Ophelia and Collette. And she was wildly, romantically in love with her husband. That was why this journey was so painful and so necessary.

Suddenly Eustacia twisted around on the box as the stage's cadence picked up tempo. She could see it behind them. They could all see it—Frank Eberson, the driver, and the six on the roof, especially the one who was whooping and pointing. At first it was a dust cloud, and then men were boiling out of it like monsters out of a dream fog, their wide-brimmed sombreros seeming to float above them. Then Frank Eberson was cussing, "Any of you damn yokels got pistols, you better clear 'em outa your pants pockets. My guess is that is some of Arango's bunch!"

"Who is Arango?" Eustacia was shouting.

Eberson took a moment to sight down his rifle barrel. He plucked at the trigger and had the satisfaction of watching one Mexican double over his horse's neck and slowly slide to the desert floor like a sack of beans. Then he glanced at Eustacia, "Got no gun, boy?"

Eustacia shook her head. She couldn't tell if the look Eberson gave her was one of pity or disgust.

From inside and outside the coach, some of the passengers were firing now, the ones on the roof who had no weapons desperately flattening themselves as if they could will themselves part of the stage. At least Eustacia wasn't doing that. It ruffled her that Eberson hadn't answered her question, so she demanded again, "Who *is* Arango?"

Eberson had emptied his rifle. Now with his enormous hands he was calmly and skillfully reloading the magazine. Because he was slightly hunched forward, his voice was close to Eustacia's ear, and she was able to catch most of what he said, despite the hammering gunfire, the driver shouting at his team, and the hollow drumming of hooves and rattle of stage.

"Near as we can figure, boy, Francisco Arango's a Mexican bandit from the northern provinces across the border. The story goes in San Bernardino that he had himself a pretty well organized ring of cattle thieves and was doin' a bang up job of terrorizin' the northern provinces. The Díaz government wasn't too pleased with him either, since this Arango also seemed to fancy

4

himself a revolutionary. So things got kind of hot for Arango, and not too long back he and his army up and crossed the border at Mexicali into Calexico. Ever since, he's been movin' steadily north, rustlin', lootin', and robbin' as he goes."

"And nobody has tried to arrest him or to drive him back into Mexico?" Eustacia asked incredulously.

Eberson cackled, "Hell, boy, of course folks have been pursuin' him, only he always tricks the law into believin' he's turned south and crossed the border again, when he's really pushed farther north. Now it looks like he's come to the Calico minin' district."

By this time Eberson had reloaded, and he twisted around again, firing methodically at the bandits. Eustacia wished he'd stop calling her "boy"; then she realized that in his eyes that was all she was—and not just because of her disguise.

Frank Eberson was in his late fifties, a man who by the way he walked and sat showed he was beginning to feel his age. He was tall, thin in a rangy manner, with a huge, surprisingly well cared for short gray beard. From what Eustacia had overheard earlier in his conversation with the driver, he had spent most of his life in southern California either involved in one part or another of the stagecoach business. Forever footloose, a stone who purposely had never wanted to grow any moss, he had frequented such southern California pueblos as Los Angeles and San Diego. But as progress had increasingly developed these areas, he had turned to the Mojave Desert, where his thinking and way of life were still unimpeded if not thoroughly accepted.

Eustacia watched mesmerized as Eberson cocked, aimed, and fired his rifle at the pursuing bandits. She was a little numb. Then slowly she began to realize that despite the firepower pouring from the stage, the Mexicans were resolutely gaining. The thought had not yet crossed her mind of what would happen to them if they were caught.

She spun frontward, scanning the Mojave floor. It seemed to be gradually sloping upward, and her eyes flicked to the distance. She could see the Calico Mountains, craggy, desolate, and multicolored in gold, blue, silver, red, and brown. *So that's how they got their name,* she thought. Eustacia realized then that the stage, with its heavy load, was losing ground because of the gradual incline as they approached the foothills.

Before she could absorb the danger they were now in, she felt the driver, who had been pressed against her, fall away from beside her. Eustacia glanced sideways and gasped. She could see the hole in the back of his neck and the blood bubbling slowly out of it. Then he was disappearing over the low iron rail, the reins slipping through slack fingers.

Instinctively, Eustacia lunged forward, grabbing at the flapping leather, nipping enough of the ends to inch her fingers downward for a more secure hold and then finally to entwine the leather through and around them. She was almost jerked out of the box as the horses began to break away at the initial slackness before she had a firm hold, but somebody hauled her back by her belt. She glanced into Eberson's face. It was as deadpan as ever.

"Nice catch, boy. Can you hang on?"

Eustacia nodded, not knowing if she could or not. The horses had kicked the driver back under the stage. A wheel bumped over the bundle, and the stage gave an unbalanced lurch. A suffocating panic seemed to well up from inside her like fog. She felt blind and deaf, and then suddenly something very cool and logical broke through. "You can't drive the stage like *that*, Eustacia," the voice inside her said. "You'll kill yourself and everyone else, too."

6

She wasn't sure whether the voice was hers or her father's, but nevertheless she buckled down to the job, remembering all the things her father had taught her about driving a team of six. She worked the reins the best she could, but the light gloves she wore were little protection from the sawing of the leather between her fingers. She also did not have the handspan of a man and was having to double up on some of the lines. But she was keeping things untangled, and the team was under control. Confident enough for the moment to examine her surroundings, she discovered that Arango's bunch was still gaining. No matter how capable she was, the Mojave was defeating her.

Eustacia was biting her lip when there came another whoop from the roof and a passenger was banging her on the shoulder and pointing into the desert on their right. Not far away she could see a train of circled freight wagons, the sand-colored canvas lashed down over their loads making them look like rising loaves of bread. Another force of Mexicans was riding down on the freighters from two directions.

"Busy, ain't he?" Eustacia heard Eberson call. He almost seemed to be enjoying himself.

Eustacia made a split-second decision, hauling the team off the road and straight across the open desert toward the wagons. It meant cutting across Arango's two-pronged attack on the freight train, and with its own pursuing party, the stage could very easily be surrounded and caught in a net. However, if the stage made it to the circled freight wagons, its chances of survival would increase dramatically. Eustacia only hoped that amid the confusion the freighters would see them coming and would be ready for them.

The stage passengers had already weighed the situation and were making adjustments. They divided themselves into three sides of a fighting machine, firing to the left and right from inside and to the rear from the roof. It reduced their firepower, but it also gave a jolt of surprise to the two pincers closing on the wagons. Nevertheless, two of Arango's men got close enough to try for the stage team. As one rushed up beside the coach, Eberson suddenly stuck out his rifle butt, knocking the bandit from his saddle as clean as if he had been wiped off by a tree branch. As the second pushed past Eustacia, she struck out with the whip. Eustacia was not skilled with whips, and the Mexican was able to wrap the flaying tip around his arm. He tugged fiercely, trying to yank Eustacia from her perch. Suddenly she let go, and the leaded handle flew hard into the Mexican's face. It struck his nose, and with a howl, he pulled back on his reins and halted, the whole parade of screaming compadres quickly passing him by.

The fighting force in front of the stage began to splinter as though darting away from annoying bees. Down the cleared lane Eustacia saw the freighters push a wagon out of position, and in a few seconds she had driven the stage through it as deftly as if threading a needle. Then she was fighting to slow the team down, pulling it around into a circle until it had made the circumference of the freighters' defense and had shuddered to a halt.

Even as Eustacia was wrapping the reins around the brake lever, the passengers and Eberson had leaped off the coach, some helping to shove the freight wagon back across the circle's gap, others finding firing positions among the freighters. Then she was running from the stage herself, dropping down beside Eberson and staring out into the Mojave.

Eberson was doing the same thing, as was the freighter on her other side. Peripherally, Eberson took notice of her, jabbing his elbow at her and speaking to the freighter. "Here's the boy that pulled it off. Done a right smart job. Boy, that there's Grant Whitman, local man. Know his daddy, Reynold, real good."

Eustacia looked at Grant Whitman, caught the quizzical look in his eyes, and quickly turned away. But in that moment, she had gotten a clear impression of him. He was perhaps thirty-four, six feet tall, the tight belly beginning to mellow a little. His hair was dark brown and starting to grow down his collar, no doubt the result of many weeks on the freighting road. His eyes were brown, creased from the sun, and quick to reflect his thoughts and emotions; she'd seen that fast enough in the look he'd given her. His nose had a bump in it, just below the bridge. She pictured him in his first little-boy fight and the obvious, inevitable result. She doubted, however, he'd lost many confrontations since. There was something very capable, intelligent, and fair about the way he met a person's gaze, in the way he carried himself. In essence, Eustacia thought, Grant Whitman was likable.

"There he is!" Eberson suddenly crowed. "There's Arango!" He stabbed his finger out at the desert.

Both Eustacia and Grant followed his gesture. The three wings of bandits were massing, sorting themselves out and lining up for another attack. All of this movement was going on in front of the man who could only be their leader. At first he had his back to the freight train, knowing he was safely out of rifle range, and then obligingly—at least for Eustacia and Grant—he turned around. Even at this distance they had a clear look at him.

Francisco Arango was of more *Indio* descent than Spanish—shorter than most of his countrymen, wiry, darker skinned, with sharp black eyes like agates. Yet from his look of iron leadership—which malevolently communicated itself across the desert—there was an aura of naked, twisted power. He was the image of a desert rat, a survivor of a harsh environment—an aimless wanderer who had molded himself into a power to be reckoned with.

"Pure cussedness, that one!" Eberson commented. "Betcha any political yearnin's he has against Díaz have to do with linin' his own pockets. Pure and simple as that."

Then Eberson noticed Grant's fixed stare, eyes squinted. "First time you had truck with Arango?" he asked.

Grant nodded.

"Wish I could say the same. I'm gettin' too old for this long San Bernardino haul with all its extra troubles. It's takin' a toll on my health."

But old or not, Eberson's was the first rifle swung up as Arango suddenly urged his horse forward, leading his army's charge.

Grant glanced sideways at the boy who had driven the stage and saw empty hands. Something felt queer, but he could not put his finger on it, didn't have time as the firing and yelling commenced. "Don't you have a pistol?" he shouted above it all.

Shaking her head, Eustacia caught the quizzical look again. Then she saw the pistol offered in his hand. She took it. She had to take it, not only for her own safety, but because the boy who had driven the stage would. Automatically she categorized it as an 1886 Smith & Wesson Frontier .44-.40 revolver—an old habit acquired from her father. Then she wondered how a freighter could have such a new gun. Usually it took a while for new weapons to filter down from the army into civilian life. Well, she reasoned, perhaps he had traded for it.

Eustacia put the thought aside—she now had to deal with her panic again. It was the same reaction she had had when she'd grabbed the stage reins. She knew the pistol shook in her hand, and she clamped down harder on the butt, forcing the cool, piercing thought to completion: *Use it and help, or you may not be alive to search for Philip.*

One of the bandits moved within range of her line of vision. Methodically Eustacia aimed, then fired. The revolver felt clumsy, but it knocked the Mexican off his horse. She blew a little air out of her mouth and concentrated on another target.

Grant, who had been watching sideways, felt the tension go out of the boy after the first shot. He knew then that the boy would be all right. Who could tell? For all any of them knew, it was the youngster's first fight. Then Grant was busy emptying his Winchester repeater and, as Arango and his men closed, his other Smith & Wesson. The blistering fire broke the charge, Arango reeling his men away just short of their horses colliding against the wagons.

"Well, there was a good one!" Eberson crowed. "Hey, Grant, what the hell these wagons carryin' that Arango wants so bad?"

"Just food and dry goods on their way into Daggett. I think three of us are continuing directly to Calico. There's no raw silver ore or ingots, as far as I know."

"Maybe Arango's supplier dried up, and he's havin' to forage for his own supper," Eberson quipped.

"Supplier?" Grant probed.

"Sure. We all figure he's got somebody who can pass in and out of Daggett or other places in the Mojave and buy supplies. Else there'd have been a lot more of this kind of business."

"Maybe," Grant agreed. "Or maybe he's finally figured out that if he can get the milk free off us, why buy the cow."

"Damn!" Eberson suddenly exploded. "The sonofabitch is goin' to hit us again!"

11

The three of them, Eberson, Grant, and Eustacia, stared out at the Mojave. Eberson's comment was being picked up all around the circle. Perhaps it was the lengthening shadows stretching across the sand like probing, grasping fingers that made the menace worse. There could be no doubt about it. Arango was massing his men as before, as though by sheer will he could ride through the wagons and the defenders. The tension in the circle was cloying and heavy.

"Well," Grant began philosophically, but with an underlying tone of toughness, "Arango has to finish us this time or leave the field. Both we and the Mexicans have used up too much firepower, and the night isn't going to help him any more than us." Then he let his voice ring out reassuringly. "We can hold him one more time! No doubt about it!"

Eberson's chuckle was low and so were his words. "Just like your daddy, Grant. You got as much guts as Reynold and the same way of talkin' people easy."

Then the surge came, the line of Arango's army devastatingly solid. The freighters threw up a thick screen of lead, pinging and spatting into the sand like dead hornets. Yet some of the Mexicans were still coming, spreading out and circling the wagons like a curling wave. They began jumping their horses between the wagons behind Grant, Eberson, and Eustacia.

Suddenly, Grant was sprinting back across the clearing, firing as he ran. A Mexican got past him, and then a second. The third Grant yanked out of the saddle by the leg. The man came off hard, rolled on his right shoulder, and scrambled to his knees and feet, flailing out with his rifle as he rocked into a steadier stance. Then he was trying to bring the rifle to his shoulder. But with a sudden downward chop of his own, Grant knocked it out of the bandit's hands. The man pulled his pistol, squeezed the trigger, and nothing happened. He tossed it aside, yanked a knife from his belt, and came charging at Grant like a bull, the long blade spearing toward Grant's midsection. Grant twisted and kicked out, catching the heel of his boot in the Mexican's stomach just below the breastbone. The man fell over like a sack of stones, gasping, then passed out.

The first Mexican on horseback was nearing Eustacia. Suddenly he catapulted himself out of the saddle and onto Eustacia's back, his hand snaking for his knife. As the weight hit and she fell face first, her breath was nearly cut off, and fear propelled her thoughts and actions into high gear. Remembering a lesson from her father, she jammed the muzzle of the Smith & Wesson underneath her left armpit and fired. The weight fell off her back, and when she struggled around, she discovered the left half of the Mexican's chest was blown apart. As she looked up, sicker than she had ever been, she saw Eberson swinging the butt of his rifle at another Mexican. It smashed into the bandit's nose, driving bone fragments into his brain.

Then it was over. By the time Eustacia, Eberson, and Grant had hauled themselves up from the sand, Arango and his army were retreating into the Mojave. None of the freighters or the stage passengers cheered. In fact, it was very still. Everyone knew it might be only a transitory victory. Then suddenly Eberson and the freight captain were yelling at once for a mount up. Everyone was scrambling and shouting. Animals that had been far from calm during the firing were outright plunging and whining as the freight wagons uncurled their circle. The stage passengers were clambering aboard, shouting congratulations or quarreling over seats. Eberson kept yelling, "Boy! Boy!"

Eustacia detached herself from the scene of the dead bandit. She ran to the coach and sprang up on the box. Eberson had already had a word with the freight captain, and he told Eustacia, "Pull in the wagon train where you can, boy. The captain says we can go on to Daggett with them."

Eustacia nodded, concentrating in the fading light on working the team and stage into position.

The place she finally chose was well ahead of Grant's wagon. Grant was standing on the foot of his box, searching the turmoil for a sign of the boy and Eberson. Finally he saw them up the line, softened by distance and dust and early evening. He tried studying the boy in the sand-colored light, the shadows deepening, the Calico Mountains silhouettes in the background.

That queer feeling was bothering him again. For a moment it flitted through his mind that when he looked at the boy he was really seeing a woman—something about the profile, a careless gesture, the way the young driver held the stage reins, the lack of a weapon. Then Grant told himself to stop being a fool, and he sat down on the wagon seat. His impression had to be a trick of light and excitement, he told himself. At last count, stage companies were not hiring women drivers. Besides, Grant had more important business at hand.

Chapter Two

Eustacia's arms and fingers were aching, and it was nearly dark by the time the stage and freight train wound its way upward through the Calico foothills to the town of Daggett. As the wagons in front of the stage began peeling away into the warehouse district, Frank Eberson said, "Keep goin'. The station is up a bit. Portage ought to have some lamps lit."

"Portage?" Eustacia asked.

"Luke Portage. He's the station manager for Daggett."

Eustacia concentrated on her driving, threading her way down the unfamiliar street. The town lights were just beginning to come on, but all she was aware of were nondescript buildings, and she was unable to pinpoint the railroad depot, the Wells Fargo office, the stamp mills, or various businesses.

Under Eberson's direction, Eustacia halted the stage in a lighted yard before a low building, the taller barn roof behind it like a wedge of cake in the dimness, the corrals spidering out from all sides. A man hurried out through the station's doorway. Eustacia had the impression he was dark haired and heavyset. He glanced at Eustacia on the box and deliberately walked around to Eberson's side. Although Eustacia could not see him clearly, she could hear him.

"What the hell is going on, Eberson?"

"Arango. Got poor old Bud. Best send someone out tomorrow to look for what's left of him. The kid here kinda took over."

"Why didn't *you* take over?"

"I was too damn busy shootin'!"

"Well, then, what about afterward? You know every job on a stage."

"I hired on as express messenger. Ah, come on, Portage, what's really eatin' you?"

"Damn it all! It's getting so if the Calico Stage Line didn't have bad luck, we'd have no luck at all! Our regular driver, he just up and quits to mine silver. This afternoon! No damn notice! I ain't got no replacement to take our Calico stage the seven miles north, so I was counting on paying Bud a little extra to take her on in for me. Then he gets himself shot!"

"Yeah." Eberson's voice was dry. "That was damn inconsiderate of him."

Portage shot Eberson a look and clamped his mouth shut.

"I'd like the driver's job, Mr. Portage," Eustacia announced, holding her voice steady and deep.

There was stunned silence. Suddenly Eustacia realized she was as surprised at herself as were Portage and Eberson. Then she remembered all the different kinds of part-time work she had taken when Philip had had job reversals. She'd learned and she'd been capable. She could handle this job. Why, she had already done it. And she knew the tremendous benefits this job could provide for her in her search. She would have an income, freedom of movement, and the opportunity to talk to many different people, any one of whom might remember her husband.

Portage finally found his voice. "You, boy? Why, I can't hire you. You're too young to have the responsibility of a stage and passengers. And I couldn't anyway, because Bill Curry has the authority to hire, not me, and he's up in Calico. Anyhow, you don't know the road from Daggett into Calico in the daytime, let alone at night."

"Now hold on, Portage," Eberson broke in. "You ain't got a lot of choices here. You have no driver for tonight. Besides, the kid has done all right. He's driven this stage safe enough, fleein' from bandits without wreckin' her, makin' good decisions for the passengers. He got us out of the open and in among the freight wagons as handy as you please. Besides, I'm willin' to ride along another seven miles and show the kid the road. Might have business with Curry myself. And come to think of it, Portage, why don't you let Curry make the final decision and take it off your back? Only he's got to see the boy, and this is the simplest way."

Portage was still thinking it over when Grant Whitman pulled his wagon alongside the stage. He'd apparently been close enough to hear part of the conversation.

Seeing, Grant, Portage exclaimed, "Well if it ain't Grant Whitman! What brings you back to the Mojave?"

"I'm hauling freight. As a matter of fact, two other freighters and I have to drive into Calico tonight. I'd be willing to follow the stage and help out if there's any trouble."

That seemed to settle the matter for Portage. Eberson knew the road into Calico, and Grant was extra insurance. "All right," he said, "it's just as well to let Curry settle this whole matter." With a bob of his head he walked back to the station.

Grant nodded, stirred his team into motion, and

17

pulled his wagon in front of the stage but to the side of the Calico road.

Eberson was instructing Eustacia. "Boy, pull this stage up the left side of the station house, then around back. The roustabout will bring the Calico stage out front. With Bud dead, Portage is goin' to have to telegraph the San Bernardino line and make arrangements about gettin' their stage back. They'll probably send one of their drivers up tomorrow."

By this time, Eustacia was master of an empty coach. Some of the passengers had already drifted into Daggett's dim streets. Those who were continuing to Calico were clustered in front of the station. As Eustacia turned the stage along the building's left side, she asked, "Who is Curry?"

"William Curry. He operates the Calico Stage Line between Calico and Daggett."

Eustacia negotiated the rest of the operation in silence, thinking how grateful she was to Grant for helping Eberson's argument along. It struck her, too, that she liked Grant, even though they'd been thrown together only for two very short periods this trying day. She would thank him for his help, Eustacia decided, when she got back out front. She was trying to say something similar to Eberson, but as she opened her mouth, he was brushing her words away with his waving hand.

"Don't waste your breath, boy. You ain't got the job yet. Besides, it was the only logical thing to do. You see, my night sight ain't what it used to be. I can spot for you, but drivin' might be risky. You keep that under your hat—you hear, boy?"

Eustacia nodded. It was a small favor to ask in return for his assistance with Luke Portage.

Eberson was off the box ahead of her, as if embarrassed, and by the time Eustacia walked around to the

front of the stage station, her intention to thank Grant
was thwarted. He seemed to have forgotten about the
boy and was in deep conversation with Eberson and
Portage about Calico. So Eustacia stood by and listened.

Grant was asking Portage, "When was the first
strike made, Luke?"

"That's right, you wouldn't have been here then,"
Portage declared. "You've been gone about seven years
now."

Grant nodded. "When Pa and I came out here to
ranch, most of this wasn't here." He gestured at the
tightly jammed buildings around them and at the Calico
stage being led into the light from the corral area.

"Where you been, anyway?" Eberson asked.

"Out seeing the world, as most restless kids do." His
eyes fell on Eustacia. She thought they looked troubled,
then she glanced away, though she listened as he
continued.

"Anyway, I always liked animals and driving, so I
picked up a trade. I'm a fair freight driver. There wasn't
much commerce going on in these parts seven years
ago."

Portage took up his story. "It was the year after
you left, in 1881, that the first strike came. Three
miners, John McBride, Larry Silva, and Charlie Meach-
am, hit silver at the head of Wall Street Canyon. McBride
had a boyhood sweetheart named Sue, and he named
the Sue Mine after her. Things didn't go smoothly at
first. The mining engineers came in and said the area
had a volcanic origin and that mining was too risky. Of
course, none of the mining capital would make an
investment. But folks kept making strikes, so eventually
some of the braver mining men decided to give the
district a shot. Now some of the best-producing mines
in California have been opened in Calico. The Silver
King is probably the richest."

19

"Isn't it named for John King, sheriff of San Bernardino County?" Grant asked.

"Yes, sir," Eberson cut in. His eyes were contemplative. "You had truck with King?"

Grant grinned. "What freighter on payday hasn't at one time or another had occasion to meet the sheriff?"

"Your daddy had some high times himself!" Eberson chuckled.

Portage, resenting the shift from himself, pushed on. "The other big producers are the Oriental, Occidental, Red Jacket, Run Over, Garfield, Bismarck, Waterloo, and Waterman in West Calico. John Daggett, lieutenant-governor, owns the Bismark and Odessa mines. Folks named this town after him."

"The town does have a bustle about it," Grant commented, his eyes sweeping the street. The town lights were completely on now, and many people still crowded the boardwalks.

There was satisfaction in Portage's tone. "It's the three large stamp mills that have done it. Our proximity to the Mojave River made them possible. Before the first one, all the ore was hauled by mule team to Oro Grande, forty miles across the desert. For lower-grade ores, the cost was out of reach, by the time you added in hauling fees and milling charges. One of our mills has built a narrow-gauge railroad into Calico via the Waterloo Mine. The biggest producers use it. The other two mills are supplied by mule team and burro pack-trains. The silver ingots are shipped via the Wells Fargo car on the Southern Pacific Railroad to San Francisco, sometimes to the U.S. Mint at 5th and Mission, and sometimes to Selby Smelting and Lead Company."

"Quite an operation," Grant commented.

"You think Daggett's got bustle," Eberson crowed, but when he saw Portage's dirty look, he interjected, "and I ain't takin' nothin' away from her—but just wait till you see Calico. That's bustle! Liveliest little one-street town! I recollect when there was only five hundred folks there. Now there's thirty-five hundred, a new schoolhouse, a newspaper called the *Calico Print*, two hundred houses, and two solid blocks of businesses. Then there's the damnedest little whorehouse—the Hurdy-Gurdy House!"

"Just about your level, Eberson," Portage said sarcastically.

Eberson looked askance. "You got loins, ain't you?" Then his expression became thoughtful. "No, maybe you don't."

Portage took a step forward, then controlled himself. "Don't forget the Chinese. They got Chinese there, too!"

There was hatred in Portage's voice. Grant couldn't decide whether it was directed at the Orientals or at Eberson for his remark.

Grant said smoothly, "None of them work in the mines though."

"You know about the Chinese, Grant," Eberson replied. "Big uproar out here on the Mojave. Nah, the Chinese are mostly domestics." His words were aimed at Portage.

The rumble of heavy wagons cut across the men's conversation, and Grant's attention swung to them. He waved the first driver past the sitting Calico stage. "You two go on ahead. I'm following the stage."

That seemed to stir Portage and Eberson into motion, too, and Eustacia prepared to go to work. Nevertheless, she had gotten a good smattering of information about her new surroundings, and it could only make her search for Philip easier.

Portage yelled, "All aboard!" and started throwing passengers' luggage into the back boot.

Eberson went into the station, returned with the mail sack, and dragged it up on the box with him.

Eustacia hesitated a moment, surveying the team of four and the coach that indeed looked very much like the San Bernardino one. The kerosene lamps attached to the front sides of the driver's box were lit.

Grant stepped up behind the boy, misinterpreting his hesitation. "Need a leg up?"

Startled, Eustacia jumped. A leg up from Grant could be disastrous. Eustacia was not *that* sure of her disguise. "No! No! I was just looking the rig over." Hastily she scrambled up the wheel, her fingers locking around the low iron railing on the driver's box as she pulled herself into position.

Grant shrugged, thinking how skittish the boy was, then walked to his wagon. As the stage started up the road, he pulled in behind it.

As they drove out of town, Eberson explained to Eustacia, "Now, the station in Calico don't go by the town name. Curry calls her Mojave Station, and you'll see why in the mornin' when you can have a good look around." Suddenly he seemed to remember something that had been on his mind, and he asked, "Hey, kid, what's your name anyway?"

"Stash. Stash Kibbe," Eustacia replied.

Despite Eberson's claim that his night vision wasn't what it used to be, he was keen enough spotting blind curves and possible trouble spots in the road. Eustacia had a sneaking suspicion that he knew the road from memory. For a little over an hour they climbed and wound their way through the folds of the Calico Mountains. Always from behind the stage came the secure *clip clop* of Grant's team and the rumble of his wagon.

Then they were there, approaching a strong globe of light that shone down Wall Street Canyon at them. As they emerged out of the gulch and into Wall Street—

the only thoroughfare in Calico—the stage and freight wagon were choked to a halt by a sizable mob.

"What the hell!" Eberson muttered.

Eustacia, as she pulled hard on the hand brake, suddenly realized why the glow of light had been so visible from the canyon. Not only were all of Calico's street lamps lit, but it looked like the entire populace was holding torches.

Eberson stood up on the box, brandishing his shotgun. "Move outa the way now! Come on, let the stage through!" A few bodies jostled aside, and Eberson ordered, "All right, Stash, get her goin' again, as far in as you can."

Eustacia released the brake, urging the team ahead with a soft clicking of her tongue. The team was skittish with all the people pressing around, and Eustacia held them on a tight rein. The stage made it halfway through Calico, Grant close behind, and then it was impossible to go any farther. The human mass was as unyielding as one of the Calico slopes. But at least, by standing up on their boxes, Eustacia, Eberson, and Grant could see what was happening.

Calico was in the middle of a hanging, stringing up a Chinese man in front of a boardinghouse that was next door to the Hurdy-Gurdy House. The rope had been flipped over the crossbar of the boardinghouse sign, the noose around the unfortunate man's neck. A Caucasian woman, struggling and kicking, was being held tightly by two burly miners in front of the Hurdy-Gurdy. She was screeching, "Yung Hen! Yung Hen!"

By the name on the boardinghouse sign, Yung Hen appeared to be the soon-deceased proprietor.

"You got any last words, Chink?" somebody snarled.

Yung Hen was calm. He was five foot six and slender, with a long queue that he wore wrapped into a bun on top of his head. His soft, floppy-brimmed hat, which he usually wore to diminish his Oriental features, lay at his feet. With an ever-so-slight raise of his shoulders, he said, in a tone clearly audible to everyone, "Go ahead. Plenty more Chinamen to take my place."

A quiet settled over the crowd, and Grant, sensing vascillation in the mob, commented loudly, "He's right, you know. You might want to keep the Chinese out of Calico, but who does your laundry and cooks in the restaurants and boardinghouses? Besides, none of them are working in the mines. They're not taking any ore away from you—not even the lowest grade, which is hardly worth a plugged nickel—let alone your jobs."

There was muttering in the crowd at the truth of his words, and again Grant picked up on it. "Come on, men, let us through. The stage is late as it is, and you are all lucky to be getting these supplies. We had a run-in with Arango."

At the mention of Arango, Yung Hen was suddenly of no further interest. The miner holding the rope dropped it, squealing, "Who wants to bother with a dumb Chinaman with that sonofabitchin' Mexican on the loose!"

"Where'd he hit you?" another called as he released the woman in front of the Hurdy-Gurdy.

The crowd began to unclog, opening a way up Wall Street for the stage and freight wagon. The people walked alongside the two vehicles, shouting questions to Grant, Eberson, and the stage passengers. Unnoticed, Yung Hen slipped the noose from his neck, coiled the hemp deftly around his elbow and arm, and then stepped off the chair he'd been standing on. Carrying the chair with his other arm, he disappeared into the boarding-house.

By the time the stage had reached Mojave Station, most everyone had heard the story and were slowly dropping back to Calico proper in search of new entertainment. Suddenly it seemed very quiet as the stage creaked to a halt in front of William Curry, who was standing in the doorway of the station. Grant continued on to a nearby warehouse.

"Well, Eberson?" Curry's voice was cool and patient.

Eustacia thought Curry and Portage were total opposites—in approach and looks. Curry was lanky, and in this light she couldn't tell if his thin hair was gray or blond. It proved to be gray.

"This here's Stash Kibbe," Eberson began. Then he slowly told the whole story of Arango and of Stash wanting the driver's job.

Curry fixed Eustacia with a long look, then he said, "Eberson's asking for the job for you. Ordinarily I wouldn't give it to someone who don't speak for himself. It shows lack of gumption. But your actions show you got that, so I'll put it this way: You're on the box, so I reckon you got the job for now. I'll give you a couple of days trial. If you do all right, then you're on permanent. It's two runs a day. Down and back in the morning, same thing in the afternoon."

Eustacia bobbed her head in thanks. At this point, she was so tired and hungry that she didn't trust herself to speak.

"Sure is quiet, ain't he?" Curry remarked. "Well, at least he won't be one of those twittery ones!"

Eberson laughed. "Could get damn boring ridin' shotgun with him."

"If the next express messenger is anything like you, he'll make up for the kid with all his own jawing! Got to hire a new man there, too."

"That's what I heard," Eberson said dryly. "How about me? I'm gettin' too old, Curry, for that long San Bernardino run."

Curry grinned. "Sure, Eberson, you're one of the

best in the business. I'd be glad to have you, even with your mouth! Let's get a drink on it."

Eberson didn't look so old jumping quickly off the box.

The roustabout, who had been hanging back behind Curry, walked up to the stage. "Harv Miller, Stash." He was older than Curry, short and bent. "I'll take the mail, get the luggage out, then drive the rig to the barn for you."

"Thanks," Eustacia whispered as she stiffly slipped to the ground. Dazed, she glanced around. Most of the crowd was gone, disappearing into the buildings back down Wall Street. Farther up from Mojave Station she could see Grant unloading supplies from his wagon into a warehouse.

Wearily, Eustacia started down Wall Street and began walking past closed stores and open dance halls and saloons. A harsh mix of raucous laughter, booming baritones, fiddle music ripping through the "Cotillion" and "Virginia Reel," and voices calling poker bets swirled around her like sand in the desert wind.

After a while, Eustacia stopped looking over swinging half doors into rooms of pooling, yellow light. She had no idea where she was going, only that she wanted a meal and a bed.

Chapter Three

Carla Maxey stood on the boardwalk in front of the Hurdy-Gurdy House, rubbing her upper arms where the miners had held her and wishing she had landed a good kick in at least one of their groins.

Carla owned the Hurdy-Gurdy. She was a friend of the Chinese man Yung Hen, had been his friend since she had become a whore—and that had been a long time ago. Her mirror never told lies. She was thirty-five and heavily fleshed, with soft shoulders and breasts. Her hair was brown and was insidiously beginning to gray on the sides and back. Her eyes were large, more round than oval, blue-gray, often steely, but more often, when she was not careful, disappointed.

Right now those eyes were watching as Wall Street emptied. Yung Hen had slipped away to lock up his boardinghouse for the night. The mob, which had churned so rapidly up the street behind the stage and freight wagon, was crumbling away like a stale slice of bread. But what was really holding her attention was the boy who had driven the stage. Carla stared hard as he mechanically walked toward her. And then, as the distance diminished, a curious blend of merriment, curiosity, and sympathy drifted across her face. The lad was no boy, Carla realized. He was a woman! Then Carla was chuckling to herself. Wasn't it like men to believe what they saw, even though they had not taken a careful look at it!

Carla's chuckle turned into a laugh, and she had to choke it down. The clothing the woman wore would have outfitted any boy, but Carla didn't think it was ever meant to deceive. There were little flaws any woman would notice. And the boy didn't walk like a male. Any man should be able to recognize that. Well, perhaps not this rough lot.

Carla was more curious and interested in the mystery than she'd been in anything else for a long time. Suddenly she began to see possibilities for amusement as she unraveled the truth. It would certainly beat the regular Hurdy-Gurdy fare, so she was ready as Eustacia's steps slowed in front of Yung Hen's boardinghouse. In her rush over from the Hurdy-Gurdy, Carla practically pounced on Eustacia, her hand snaking out and grabbing her upper arm.

"Young man, you don't want to go in there! No, you need something to wash the dust down, and some music to bring up your spirits—and I might even have a nice flaky meat pie to pop into you. I'm a good cook when I give myself half a chance." Carla patted her padded belly. "You need a friend, and I'm gonna be yours."

Eustacia was overwhelmed, shaken out of her weary daze, too surprised to object as the woman swept her into the Hurdy-Gurdy next door. Face and name came together when she realized this was the woman who had tried to defend the Chinese man. Eustacia relaxed a little. The woman couldn't be all bad, certainly not the epitome of a woman of ill repute, as proper society often viewed such ladies.

Despite her weariness, Eustacia's curiosity was aroused as Carla propelled her toward the bar. She had never been in a brothel before, and her neck might have been on a swivel for all the looking she was doing. A smug look quickly passed across her face as Eustacia thought how she was behaving right in character for a callow youth.

Carla was openly grinning. She saw both sides of the situation, enjoying the young woman's private joke, as well as the one Carla was simultaneously playing on her.

"Jess." Carla beckoned to her bartender. "I want two pours from the best bottle of Kentucky bourbon," she said, adding just to make sure he understood, "my personal bottle."

Jess looked at her as though she'd gone queer, then shrugged. It was none of his affair if she broke from her longstanding rule of never sharing her private stock with the clientele.

Carla's grin twitched a little at the corners. No matter how much she wanted some fun at Eustacia's expense, she couldn't let her swallow down the same rotgut her hard-drinking miners did. From long practice their stomachs had acquired iron linings.

Carla passed a glass to Eustacia, who took it absently, putting it to her lips the same way, her eyes full with everything around her. Deciding it was only fair to let her have a good look, Carla inclined her head toward one of the customers who had been trying to get Carla's attention.

The Hurdy-Gurdy was essentially a long narrow building with a second-story gallery. Its walls were dark, rough wood, bare except where huge squares of various-colored fabric had been nailed, a crude attempt

29

at feigning tapestries. The bar ran along one narrow end. Along the sides were tables and chairs. The center of the room was reserved for dancers and the poor soul of a man who cranked out tunes on an impressive but wheezy hand organ. No doubt the hurdy-gurdy instrument and the dancing, which provided a thin veneer of respectability, accounted for the establishment's name. But the real business of the Hurdy-Gurdy House went on in the gallery above, which was curtained off into stalls, each stall a different color, the fabrics lightly rustling and fluttering in the draft like medieval ladies' scarves.

Eustacia had expected to be left alone once Carla brought her inside, but as she took a second sip of bourbon, suddenly feeling warm and less tired, she realized the woman was waiting beside her. "Thank you." Eustacia gestured with her glass. Eustacia usually only drank on holidays and at family occasions, and then not more than a glass or two of wine, but tonight the bourbon was working wonders on a sore body. She was grateful.

"Now for that spot of meat pie. You wait here," Carla ordered.

Carla swung around the end of the bar and opened a small door. It led into a small lean-to, obviously added on later, which Carla used as her kitchen. It contained the best wood-burning stove she could get shipped into Calico, cupboards cheerfully decorated with crockery, and a small cot. Many an evening, feeling bleak within herself, Carla had sought the room's warmth, security, separateness, and normalcy.

Palming a dishtowel, Carla pulled a tin out of the warming oven. In it were the remains of the pie she had had for supper, still warm and juicy with gravy. She arranged it on a plate with a thick slice of bread and some canned fruit. Then she whisked back out to the bar, closing the door softly behind her as though the place was some secret part of herself. She gestured at Eustacia. "Come along and eat."

Carla led the way to her back table—her business table where neither girl nor customer ever sat—and she quickly set a place and laid the plate down.

With her first bite of food chewed and swallowed, Eustacia asked Carla, "How does this place work?"

Carla's eyebrows arched. This was going to be more fun than she had thought. The "lad" was playing right along.

"On a percentage," she replied. "The girls who come here to dance get a share of the bar tab and the dance fee charged these yokels." The last term was said with affection. Then Carla gestured up at the gallery. "If the girls turn a trick, they share their money with me."

"Do the women live here?"

Carla shook her head. "I ain't the kind to maintain a house. That's a lot of work. The girls all have their own little cribs and probably work for themselves on the side. That's all right with me. I only care about what happens on my premises."

Eustacia thoughtfully chewed her meat pie. It was spicy and filling. It seemed Carla's upstairs business was profitable; a leisurely stream of traffic rolled up and down the stairwell. Some of the girls looked a little worn, bruised around the edges, but most were fresh-faced enough. Eustacia suddenly realized how the day had mushroomed her horizons, and for some reason that made her think of the near hanging.

"Why did they want to hang the Chinese man?" Eustacia asked.

Carla looked disgusted. "Bigots." She swept her hand at the miners. "The Chinese have never been popular in California, despite the fact we brought them

31

in to build our railroads. Maybe it's because they make something of themselves and survive no matter how little they've got. Lot of mining camps made up rules, not allowing the Chinese to cull out even the lowest grade ore, because somehow they'd make money on it. Now you take Yung Hen." She tapped her finger on the table. "I've known him a long time. Helped me out of a bad spot, he did, in the very beginning."

Carla made a wry face, then found her story again. "Yung Hen is *so visible*. He owns, actually owns, that boardinghouse next door. He's grubstaked many a miner and fed lots more till they got on their feet. But jealousy sets in—actually seeing a yellow man making a success of himself. So, enough liquor and a little boredom, and half the town's ready to string up the Chinaman." Carla laughed. "Everything'll be all right from now on! Steam's off the surface of the pot. Yung Hen took the wind out of their sails when he told them he didn't care if they hung him. Canny fellow. He rules the other Orientals with an iron hand. There's forty Chinese all together in Calico."

"Calico got it's name from the mountains, didn't it? I was noticing them on the ride in."

"In a manner of speaking." Carla patted Eustacia familiarly on the arm and winked with exaggerated slowness. It threw her face into a clownish half leer.

Eustacia had the feeling she was supposed to feel like a fellow conspirator in some uproariously funny game. Amazed, she diplomatically shifted her arm out of reach and settled a little farther back in her chair.

Carla out and out grinned. It turned her half leer into a full one. Then she straightened her face much as a drunkard does his gait. "Wish I'd had the liquor concession on that meeting. It seems that after several families settled here and after it was a proven fact the ore deposits were rich, the folks wanted a post office.

You have to petition the federal government, which means making out an application. On the application you have to put the settlement's name, only this camp didn't have one. So there was a first meeting where no one could agree. There had to be another, and this time someone got smart and brought a keg of liquor, which was promptly opened and liberally sampled. The choices for the camp's name eventually boiled down to Silver Gulch, Silver Canyon, Buena Vista, and Calico. Now, the liquor was running close to bottom, and all of those left standing favored Calico, declaring the mountains reminded them of 'a purty piece of Calico.' So J. A. Delameter wrote the name on the application and sent it to Washington, and the town got a post office."

Carla swung her gaze over the room. More couples were sitting than dancing, and traffic was slowing on the stairs. It meant the evening was getting late, winding down. She'd be closing up pretty soon.

Absently, Carla added, "James Stacy's the postmaster. He's got himself an assistant, a dog called Dorsey."

"How can he have a dog for an assistant?" Eustacia was truly surprised. It was one more bizarre fragment of the day.

"You'll see if you're staying around at all. *Are you staying around?*"

Eustacia nodded. "I got the job driving the Calico stage."

"Oh, you did now, huh!" Carla could feel the laughter bubbling inside her like bicarbonate of soda bubbles and pushing outward against her ribs at the strains of her corset. She was having a hard time not howling her head off.

Innocently, Eustacia continued, "Frank Eberson swore for me, even though I'm so young."

"He did, that old coot!" Carla couldn't keep it in.

33

The horselike belly laugh exploded over the wheezy hand organ music.

Eustacia, puzzled, figured it had something to do with Eberson and Carla's relationship.

Carla sputtered to a halt and shot Eustacia a sheepish glance. It was obvious the poor woman did not suspect she'd been discovered.

"Well, now," Carla recovered, "if you're going to be living in Calico, you ought to know something about her. There's a few names that'll serve you in good stead. The town doctor is A. R. Rhea, and we got us a registered nurse, Mary Ryan. That fellow Delameter I mentioned before, well he's practically responsible for creating this town. He was one of the first miners in the district, but his main interest was freighting—still is."

Suddenly Eustacia realized that Delameter was the name she'd seen stenciled on the side of the warehouse where Grant Whitman had been unloading his wagon earlier this evening. She wondered where he had gone afterward. She didn't think she'd seen him come in here, but then she had been busy eating and listening.

Carla was talking through Eustacia's thoughts. "Delameter abandoned mining to bring in supplies for the miners. He started the stage line between Calico and Daggett, though Bill Curry has it now. He still has a part interest in a feed yard and livery stable here in Calico, and he financially backed John Overshiner so he could start the *Calico Print*. Delameter even writes for the paper some."

"Is there a good store?" Eustacia asked.

"Joseph Miller has a general merchandising—and a delivery wagon with two of the slowest mules in history, named January and February. We call them the Lightning Express. Their top gait is a walk." Then, as if mention of the store had further jogged her memory,

Carla added, "The Globe Restaurant on the other side of Yung Hen's is a good place to eat."

"I heard down in Daggett that Calico has a new school."

"New as of '84. Opened in October of that year. Miss Mamie Mooney's the teacher." Carla had a bemused smile on her lips as she slowly shook her head. "Unfortunately, Calico is trying to become more than just a silver camp. Take for instance the folks that want to change Wall Street to Main Street. *Take some of the audacity out of the town is what they really want to do!* Sure it's pretentious to call the narrow and only street in town after that wide avenue in big, bustling New York! But then, hell, there's just as much money on this street as there is on the other!"

Carla took a breath, then continued, "If the street name gets changed, then this place and the saloons and cribs are on their way out, too." Then she laughed. "Look at these rough old souls. Place would practically have to burn down around their ears before they'd realize something different was happening."

Then she seemed to backtrack momentarily. "You know, there's a reason for only one long street in town. There's only room enough for one. Calico is built on a narrow, level plateau on the south slope of the Calico Mountains."

Eustacia nodded as Carla's words flowed around her, giving her unspoken encouragement. There was no doubt about it. The woman was a wealth of information, and eventually there might be mention of Philip. For now Eustacia would ask no questions, but just let Carla talk, while she got a footing in her new environment.

"Politics here, well it's like a party," Carla chattered. "The brass band and the glee club turn out, and folks string Chinese lanterns across the street and nail extra torches to the buildings. Probably the best blow was also back in '84. The presidential election was on—Cleveland and Hendricks against Blaine and Logan—and Calico was helping elect a congressman as well."

Eustacia nodded wearily, glancing around the quieting room. The hurdy-gurdy man was playing something sad and slow. She wondered vaguely if Carla, so busy with her chatter, had noticed closing time was approaching. As if Carla read her thoughts, Eustacia got her answer.

Scraping her chair back and balancing in one hand Eustacia's plate with her glass on top of it, Carla pointed with the other hand at a man slipping in the door and sweeping the room with a satisfied look. "That's Mr. Tucker. He's assistant superintendent at the Run Over Mine and Mill. If he's here, it means it's time to close up. He spot-checks in here a couple of times a week to make sure his boys have cleared out when they should, so they can give him a full day's work."

Eustacia watched Carla's broad back rock away from her. A smile drifted over her lips. The woman was kind, and she liked her.

Carla whispered something to both the bartender and the hurdy-gurdy player, and then slipped into the kitchen. Jess, the bartender, immediately began clapping corks into bottles, the hurdy-gurdy man breaking into a fast and bumpy jig. It must have been a regular signal, Eustacia thought, because the miners started trickling out the door. Eustacia roused herself and fell in step. She still had to do something about a bed.

Carla, coming out of the kitchen, saw her "young man" join the departing vanguard, and she nearly killed herself crossing the room, slipping in a slick of spilled drink and barking a shin against a chair leg. Part of her hurry stemmed from guilt. She couldn't let the woman out on the streets by herself at this hour! But also, fun was fun, and her curiosity had to be satisfied. So, looking like a floundering whale maneuvering across the dance floor, she finally caught up to Eustacia, her palm clamping down on Eustacia's shoulder. "Now where you think *you're* going?"

"To find a bed."

"You've got a bed right here. There's a couple of cubicles that haven't been used this evening. You can have one of those cots. Besides, Yung Hen locked up ages ago. It won't be so bad. It's only for one night."

The last miner slipped into the night, and Carla nudged the door shut with her toe, turning Eustacia back into the room.

Repleted with food and drink, suddenly exhausted, and looking, none too clearly, at the day of work ahead, Eustacia decided Carla was right. "I'd be most appreciative."

"Done!" Carla swept toward the stairs, Eustacia bobbing behind like a cork in her wake.

Carla led the way to the second floor, past several fluttering, curtained stalls, then stopped in front of a yellow one. She jerked back the fabric in two hard tugs, the material sliding noiselessly on its rod. Grandiously, she waved Eustacia inside, practically treading on her heels as she followed her in, then whipped the curtain shut again. Provocatively, she placed a palm on one well-padded hip, arched her body in the age-old stance, and smiled. Her eyes twinkled at the shock, surprise, and confusion chasing across Eustacia's face, and she wondered how long the woman would pursue her ruse.

Eustacia backed up a little, which put her even closer to the cot in the cramped quarters. Then she stopped, suddenly realizing the possible danger of proximity. "Ah, Carla," she stammered out, "it's not that I don't appreciate . . . but today was a long day, and tomorrow will be longer. I'm tired," she finished lamely.

"Now, no healthy young man ever gets *that* tired! You look like a fine specimen to me!"

Eustacia was blushing as she scrambled for another excuse. Suddenly she blurted out, "I've never done it before!"

Carla maternally patted the "young man's" sleeve, and Eustacia, as if she had been singed by fire, jerked it back out of reach.

"Now then, you've come to just the right place," Carla pitched, insinuatingly moving her body. "A young man's first time ought to be the very best and the most carefully done. It ought to be with someone of expertise. I qualify there. Now come along, duckling." Exaggeratedly, she reached for Eustacia.

Eustacia stumbled backward onto the cot, saw herself caught in her own trap, gulped, then held up a restraining hand. "Wait! Wait, Carla! There's something you ought to know."

"Oh?" It was a raspy purr, pitching up at the end.

"You see, I agree with you, but there is still one problem."

"There is?" She repeated the same purr.

"I'm not a young man. I am a woman." In her desperation, Eustacia's voice was shriller than normal.

"Yes," Carla said calmly. The mirth was still behind her eyes, deep in her throat. Casually she doffed Eustacia's hat.

Eustacia was stunned, then she saw the humor of the entire evening and began to laugh. "You knew! You knew all the time."

"Yep." Carla exploded with laughter, her sides shuddering against her ribs until her breath came in tight, sharp stitches, and the pain put a gulping end to her merriment. "Oh my, honey," she finally whispered.

"Eustacia Kibbe."

"Well, then, Eustacia honey, you've given me a

good time, and I thank you. Eventually I want to hear the whole story of how you got yourself into this predicament. But for now, get some sleep. Driving a stage is hard work. And don't you fret none. I meant what I said at the start about being your friend. Your secret is safe with me. As far as I'm concerned, any time a woman can beat a man at his own game, I'm for her!"

"Thanks, Carla." Eustacia started pulling off her mackinaw jacket.

"You want anything, I'll be down in the kitchen tonight. I'll get you up in plenty of time to make your run." Then Carla was out of the cubicle, twitching the yellow fabric back in place. Her chuckle drifted back up the hall like bubbling water.

Grant Whitman, who was sitting on the edge of the cot in the stall next door, one leg in his trousers and one out, suddenly felt vindicated. He had been right after all in his first impression of the stage driver. But what was the woman up to? He decided that Eustacia Kibbe's secret was also safe with him—for a while, at least, until he figured out her game.

Grant quietly stuffed his other leg into his pants. The girl he had been with had long ago left him sleeping. Now he was going to have to sneak out of the closed building, just like a schoolboy caught in the wrong place at the wrong time. Grant winced at the deflating thought, then began his tiptoe descent.

Chapter Four

It was three days since the stagecoach and freight train had escaped Francisco Arango, and the Mexican bandit was still angry. Under the escarpment of rock where he sat, knees pulled up to his chest, it was cold, and the long shadows on the desert beyond were puddling together like slow-flowing ink. For a moment, he wished he were back in the northern provinces of Mexico, even in a poor goatherd's squalid mud and straw hut, with a pot of beans bubbling over the fire, and a woman, even a fat one, to serve him. Then he laughed silently at himself. He must be chewing too much root to want to go back to the rat hole he had fled. Yet how could he have surrounded himself with and trained such a large pack of jackals and still lose a stage and a wagon freight train? He grunted in disgust as the pinches of light from the campfires of his men began to flare to the left and right of him along the rock base.

Then he saw Philip Kibbe, the fair-haired gringo, coming to him out of the gloom. A smile bent Arango's lips, cynical and foxlike. The gringo was a fool who took Francisco Arango for something better than he was. But the fool was necessary. He was Arango's arm to the outer world from the fortress he had made of the Mojave.

"*Hola, Emil!*" Arango called, suppressing a snicker. The Mexican name was an alias Philip had chosen, and Arango agreed to use it to make the man feel comfortable and accepted—a compadre.

Philip Kibbe stooped underneath the escarpment and sat down next to Arango, his eyes also on the desert. He saw wonderful pictures in the shadow paintings—a form that resembled a Spanish conquistador, a peasant man bent over with a bundle of sticks, a young girl, willowy and insubstantial and therefore beautiful. "Lovely, isn't it?"

Arango saw nothing but sand and brush and darkness. "You have the mind of an artist," he said flatly, though to him that was no compliment.

Fitting his self-image as a poet and a dreamer of great things, Philip Kibbe was tall and slender with curly blond hair, blue eyes, and a quick laugh. He was also easygoing and could be extremely patient, which made it easy for him to weather Arango's rages and soothe his anger. After all, he often reminded himself, all great men like Arango were filled with such energy.

"You don't want a fire?" Philip asked, pulling his jacket collar tight around him.

"I suppose eventually it will be forced upon me, and then I will have to look upon that scum."

"One can only lament a miscalculation for so long."

"Stupid jackass-eared rabbits of men!" Arango muttered, spitting into the sand. His comment was meant to include this gringo who fancied himself Emil, though Philip remained blissfully oblivious.

"There will be fresh meat tonight. Some of the *hermanos* have snared small animals."

"No doubt it will be the flesh of a rat," Arango remarked bitterly.

Philip chuckled, appreciating Arango's wry humor.

"Tell them, Emil, that *mañana* I want fresh beef. Why are we camped on this rancho if we cannot take cows?"

Since Arango had invaded the Mojave, he had often camped on the outlying acres of several ranches, stealing cattle as he saw fit to feed himself and his army. Some of the ranchers remained totally ignorant of his presence, others were aware but chose to ignore it. The rest he had intimidated, brutally stripping their chicken coops and gardens if they objected.

"I have been sitting here making plans," Arango broached.

"Of course, to help the people against Díaz's harshness!" Philip was eager.

Arango was glad he had delayed his campfire. Philip could not see his humorless smile. Arango remembered when he and a few compadres had surrounded this naive gringo, who was on his way to Calico intent on being a miner, though he did not know the first thing about mining or the desert. They had intended to rob him of his supplies and whatever was in his pockets. Arango, half tongue-in-cheek, had expounded on all his political reasons for such petty pilfery. Philip had stunned him. Caught up in Arango's rhetoric about how he was going to break the back of the Díaz government and improve the lot of his countrymen, Philip had willingly turned over his possessions and had begged to join his ranks.

Arango's first reaction had been to laugh. He was flattered that his poor peasant words had had such an effect. Then, too, he immediately saw the vistas Philip could open to him. In short order, Philip became a procurer of guns and supplies for Arango.

As for Philip, though he knew his wife and daughters idolized him, he cut all ties with them. At heart, he was a romantic, an adventurer, a knight—the very qualities, he believed, that had earned him his family's adoration. He saw himself as a dashing friend of the revolution, and he had adopted the name Emil to fit the image. Philip had taken eagerly to the role of Arango's procurer of supplies and had proved himself extremely effective. This was ironic, since he had failed in most of his business enterprises in San Bernardino and had often been forced to rely upon the additional income Eustacia had brought in over the years to carry their family through until he had a new prospect.

"This new plan should help the people much, Emil," Arango said dryly. "I want to raid the Wells Fargo railroad car that carries the silver ingots from Daggett."

Philip's eyebrows arched. "You are talking about stopping a Southern Pacific train, Francisco, and dealing with many guards. Also, not every train leaving Daggett carries the silver. We would need much information—the timing of the shipments of raw ore from Calico down to the stamp mills in Daggett, how long the process takes, how often an express car is loaded and leaves, and, of course, on which train." Then Philip stopped and sucked in his breath. "You want me to do more this time than just give you supplies! You want me to obtain all that information!"

"Sí."

Philip could hardly believe his good fortune. At first he was silent, and then like an overexcited puppy jumping at his beloved, he was stammering, struggling with a rush of gratitude. He saw Arango's hand flick at him in the dimness, and determinedly he clamped his lips shut.

"Go bring me food now, Emil."

Philip slid out from under the escarpment and approached a Mexican with a spitted, cooked animal.

Arango took his dinner, careful not to look at it. He

stared into the dark distance, envisioning first a butchered cow and then a car of silver ingots. What did it matter what the leader, the *jefe*, ate tonight?

Unfortunately, it mattered a great deal to Reynold Whitman, Grant's father, when he discovered the next morning that he was providing someone's table. Out riding range, he was drawn by the vultures. They led him to a heap of horns and hooves and offal. Disgusted, he didn't even bother to shoot the coyote that was dragging off a length of intestine. Carefully, he followed the trail of five shod horses—no doubt four riders and a packhorse. It brought him across the width of his land to the shallow rock gullies. And then, appearing as bold as brass, though he was actually surprised, he rode into the middle of Arango's camp. The sentries, equally startled, bristled rifles like porcupines, making a good show of crying out to each other in Spanish to cover their lack of preparedness.

Arango was not fooled. His men had come to rely too much on the oppressiveness of the Mojave to deter anyone intent on hunting them down. There would have to be drills and then more drills. *"Estúpidos!"*

Reynold Whitman, glancing around at the established camp, idly wondered how long he had been providing for the bandits. Then he spotted his cowhides pegged out on the sand, and he was angry. He isolated Arango with an accusing finger as narrow as a wand. "I know who you are. I want no part of you. I don't want you feeding yourselves on my cattle. Get the hell off my land, you damn desert rat!"

Arango's face showed nothing, though behind the glasslike eyes contempt rose like bile. He looked at the American on the horse and saw an old man, straight and gaunt with gray stubble over the square jaw. He saw someone who annoyed him with his tracking skill and his high-handedness.

Arango did not say a word. He barely moved, except for the gentle wave of his rifle barrel. He pulled the trigger, shrugged ever so lightly, and then turned and walked back to the escarpment.

Those who were closest to the old American did not wait. The bullet was killing Whitman, but it had not knocked him out of the saddle. Many hands clawed him out, and then began the stripping and dividing up of his belongings. Reynold Whitman died staring at the pegged cowhides, his lips dried by sand.

Arango stood in front of the escarpment, watching his jackals finish. Philip joined him and cautiously asked, "What happened?"

"Meddlesome thing. No importance." Arango stepped away and called to his men, "We move. Pack up the fresh meat, all else." He saw one man reach for a peg at the corner of a hide. "Leave it. It is no good unless dried. Besides, it is a tombstone, a reminder to other ranchers of our power." Then he turned to Philip. "Now I must pick four good men. *Not* the ones who allowed the old gringo to track them."

When the four stood before him, he said very succinctly, "You are to guard our back trail. You will kill anyone who crosses it. *Comprenden?*"

"*Comprendemos.*"

They stood staunchly, like four wooden soldiers, until the dust of their compadres was only a thin wisp of smoke.

Grant Whitman left Calico on horseback only a few minutes after Eustacia drove the stage down Wall Street and dipped into the canyon gulch south for Daggett. Grant was bent on visiting his father. During the past three days, he had been tied up hauling freight between Calico and Daggett, and this was the first opportunity he had had to make the visit.

Grant had not seen Reynold since he had left the Mojave area seven years ago to join the army. He and his father had a good relationship, and they had kept in touch by mail. But though he loved the ranch and the home his father had scraped out of the Mojave Desert, Grant just didn't think he had what it took to be a rancher, especially a Mojave Desert rancher. His father had understood, so Grant had gone to the army with his blessing.

Grant had excelled at his job, working himself into the intelligence sector. That was really why he was back in the Mojave. He had been assigned to the area to determine the movements and possible threat of Arango. Working as a freight driver gave him freedom of movement in a district he knew very well, without exposing his true mission. Now Grant was riding out to visit his father and to see if, somewhere along the way, he could pick up Arango's trail.

When Grant reached his father's ranch house and found him gone, he was not suprised. Reynold often left at first light to ride range, thus escaping some of the Mojave's heat. Casually, Grant swung his mount onto his father's trail and followed. He didn't start to get concerned until he saw the vultures, then all of a sudden nothing felt right. Somehow he knew it never would again.

Grant reined in at the heap of horns and hooves; the offal was all gone by now, carried off by scavengers. Obviously, someone had butchered Whitman cattle—by the looks of the debris and tracks, enough to feed many mouths. Arango and his bandits? Suddenly Grant's stomach churned as he imagined his father running into that pack. After the attack on the freight train, Grant had a healthy respect for the Mexican, and he knew more could be learned through guile and from a watchful distance than through direct confrontation. But his father would have been angry. Suddenly, Grant was spurring his horse into a headlong rush up the trail.

At the second flock of circling vultures, he slackened his pace. His destination was abundantly clear, and whatever had transpired in the rocks ahead was already done and over with. Grant stopped, dismounted, wrapped the reins around an outcropping, and pulled his rifle. He levered a shell into the chamber but carried it muzzle down. If he was walking into Arango's camp, it was probably abandoned, since he detected no sentries. If Arango had gone, he probably would have left a rear guard, but they would not have remained close to the old camp.

Grant saw it all at once, as though his father was the picture and the cowhides the frame. In a daze, he walked into the camp, his bootheels scraping through the sand. He knelt beside the body of his father, closed the eyes, and brushed the exploring insects from the face and torso. Looking down at Reynold, a rush of memories came back to him—all the things they had done and said, and the words he now would never be able to say. Grant felt the anger and pain building within him, but the tears would not come. His eyes were as dry and he felt as empty as the desert around him.

Grant got to his feet and went back to his horse, returning with his saddle blanket. He flipped out the roll and wrapped his father's body in it, hooding the head; then he stepped away. "I'll be back, Dad. I'll be back in a little while," he whispered.

He swung a glance around the camp, saw the string of many abandoned campfires along the escarpment, and knew he had been right about Arango. This bivouac told him one of the ways the bandit was surviving on the Mojave.

With so many riders, the trail was a clear one.

Grant followed it with caution. There was no telling how large a rear guard Arango had left—not with the confusion of so many hoofprints. They led north brazenly across the open sand in the direction of Daggett and Calico, then abruptly turned east as though to swing around the Calico Mountains beyond Mule Canyon and the borax mines. It seemed like a good area in which to hide.

Grant never got a chance to follow his hunch. Without warning a shot crashed out, nipping at the narrow brim of his hat, blowing the hat one way and fragments of felt into an eye. He hauled his horse broadside to the blast, pulled his right leg over the pommel, and dropped lightly to the ground, rifle in hand. Somewhat protected by the horse's shifting bulk, his eye blinking with tears, he scanned for cover and spotted a clump of desert grass and a shallow dune, a mere ripple of the floor. Dropping and rolling, he got behind it, then inched his way upward a little so he could see over the top.

The Mojave was silent and unyielding. Grant stared so hard that his vision compressed tunnellike as he willed someone to make a mistake and show himself. The terrain was nearly devoid of cover, a light-brown table cloth, until a quarter of a mile ahead it corrugated into overlapping folds of shallow dunes, the gateway to the mountains beyond. The Mexicans were probably in the dunes.

Suddenly Grant noticed a small bunch of desert grass, not unlike his own, fifteen feet in front of the dunes. He studied the edges of the grass, trying to pierce right through its drab olive screen. After a few minutes he was rewarded. He saw a dark smudge in the grass—a sombrero, no doubt. The Mexican was probably lying behind the grass in a shallowly dug trench, waiting for someone to pass nearby for an easy and deadly shot.

It was the only target Grant had, and he had to hit it if he was to get through the rear guard and the gateway.

Grant slid the rifle barrel over the rim of his little dune, sighted, then thought better of the shot. His bullet would have to arch upward over the dune and then downward toward the Mexican. It was an improbable hit. So with a muttered, "What the hell," Grant sprang to his feet, steadied his stance, took aim, and pumped three shells at the grass and sombrero. Two things happened next. A fusillade from the dunes beyond the target whistled in like Fourth of July rockets, falling short but churning up enough sand to reduce visibility. The Mexican erupted from his trap, whirling like a leaf caught in the wind, then collapsed in a heap. Grant was never sure whether it had been his own shot or the return fusillade from the other bandits in the dunes that had cut the man down.

Then it was over as suddenly as it had begun. The Mojave was silent, the echo of gunfire a distant rumble. Grant lay on his back, rifle across his chest, panting, listening. Nothing. He rolled over and looked over his ripple of sand at the gateway. They were gone. He did not know how he was so sure, except that he had this huge sensation of inner emptiness.

Grant stood up. His horse had trotted behind him but remained still, waiting like a good army horse. Grant strode purposely toward him as he reloaded the spent shells he had used. Then he shoved his rifle in the scabbard, mounted his horse, and put him into a gallop. He passed the dead bandit without a glance, then soared through the folds of sand like a rodent-hunting hawk.

At first the trail of the rear guard was clear, born of

hasty flight. Then it just fell to pieces, rubbed out in many places. And when he stumbled upon portions of it, it was so badly confused that he was forced to give up. With enough effort he could possibly reconstruct it, but he didn't have the time. There was his father lying behind him, awaiting a funeral.

Grant turned his horse around and rode back to Arango's former camp. He securely tied the body of his father across the back of his own horse, since Arango's people apparently had stolen his father's mount, and began walking toward the stage road between Calico and Daggett.

Eustacia Kibbe, with Frank Eberson on the box beside her, wasn't more than a mile and a half out of Daggett on her way back to Calico when she saw Grant Whitman standing in the middle of the road, a bundle across the back of his horse. As she braked, he moved to the side. He looked more than just tired.

Eberson leaned over the side railing, the stage and harness still jingling. "What's the trouble, Grant?"

"Arango and his bunch shot Dad."

"Goddamn! Goddamn! Reynold . . ." And then he didn't say any more.

Grant walked to the back of the stage, past the stares of the curious passengers. He tied his horse to the rear boot, then came back to the box on Eustacia's side. "Could I please ride up with Frank and you?" Woman or not, the driver had the say about who rode in the box. Eustacia nodded.

Grant climbed up beside Eberson. No one spoke while Eustacia released the brake and got the stage started up the grade again.

Finally Eberson asked, "How you think it happened, Grant?"

Briefly Grant told the story. When he finished,

Eberson shook his head. Suddenly Eberson looked older, more tired, and Eustacia began to believe the things he had said about his age.

"Well, that woulda done it for Reynold. He was real sensitive about his cows. Said it had took too much hard work to scrape out what he had for someone else to reap his profit."

Grant nodded. "I've learned something about Arango, too. People always thought he had someone supplying him out in the desert, and undoubtedly he still does. But if he was hiding out on our ranch, eating off it, then he could be doing the same to all the other ranchers in this area. Somebody ought to know something."

"Makes sense to me," Eberson agreed.

Eustacia suddenly spoke up. "Why don't you talk to Carla Maxey at the Hurdy-Gurdy, Grant? She knows a lot about Calico."

Then Eustacia regretted her impulse. Grant fixed her with a look she couldn't read, and it made her uneasy—made her hope she hadn't done anything to get Carla into trouble.

The arrival of the Calico stage always was a high point in the silver camp, but today as Eustacia drove up Wall Street, it downright stopped regular business. Even the crazy man who lived in the lean-to near the King Mine and regularly chased the stage with a wheel barrow, yelling "Free bus to the Hyena House!" broke stride and stuttered into silence at the sight of the body-bearing horse swinging loosely behind the coach. Word was sent up ahead of the stage for Dr. Rhea, and when Eustacia halted the team of four in front of Mojave Station, he was waiting.

Grant jumped off the box, meeting Dr. Rhea over by his horse. The doctor had the hooded part of the saddle blanket pulled back and had just finished manipulating Reynold Whitman's eyelids. He met Grant's gaze as he tucked the hood back around the dead man's face.

"I'm not telling you anything you don't already know, Grant."

"No." Grant unlooped the reins from the stage and started walking back down Wall Street, the doctor falling in step beside him.

"You stop in a minute before going to make arrangements, and I'll sign the death certificate. What was it, or do I have to make an examination?"

"Gunshot."

Dr. Rhea's eyebrows arched.

"Arango." Grant's voice was bitter. The numbness was wearing off, he suddenly realized. Although he would watch himself very carefully now, making sure to carry out his orders and his duty, the hunt for Arango had suddenly become personal.

An ice wagon went by them, the team splashing through the open sewage ditch, throwing the foul half-liquid on Dr. Rhea's pant legs. "Dammit all! When will these people learn about bettering their sanitary conditions? You'd think the typhoid epidemic of '83 would have taught them something!"

"What, Doc?" Grant asked, surfacing from his own thoughts and plans.

"Typhoid, my man. The germ, whatever you want to call it—infective agent—enters the body through the mouth, usually in contaminated water or milk—some even say food. The agent usually gets into the water or milk from the excrement of a sick or convalescing individual. That means if you have an unsatisfactory sewage system—like here—the chances of raw excrement getting into the water supply are good. Get a sanitary sewage system and you help eliminate the problem.

"You know, it wasn't until '80 that C. J. Eberth recognized the typhoid bacillus. It took a man named Gaffkey in '84, isolating it in a pure culture, to give us knowledge about diagnosing it and . . ." Dr. Rhea saw Grant was not listening, so he stopped talking. What should Grant Whitman care about what was in the medical journals? Grant was about to bury his father.

Eustacia, off the box, stood watching Grant's progress down Wall Street. Something bothered her a great deal, as much as the look he had given her earlier. She suddenly felt surrounded by secrets, and she shivered.

"Penny for your thoughts?" Eberson asked.

"Oh, it just seems—I mean I have this feeling— that Grant is just more than an ordinary freighter."

"Could be. But then, if I was you I'd leave well enough alone." Eberson strolled off to talk to Harv Miller, who was leading the team and stage away.

Eustacia pulled her eyes from the street and looked down along the plateau. She knew in her heart that Frank Eberson was right. After all, she had something to hide herself.

Suddenly Eustacia realized what she was looking at—the whole reason William Curry had called the Calico way station Mojave Station. From where she stood, she could see the dry lake out on the desert, the blue thread of the Mojave River, and in the distance, the San Bernardino Mountains. It opened her up inside, and for a moment Eustacia forgot to worry.

Chapter Five

Eustacia's stomach was grumbling, and with a sigh she tore herself from the view of the Mojave and began walking down Wall Street. Today for some reason Calico and its long, dusty, narrow street teemed with even more life than usual. She found herself dodging mule-drawn ore wagons, which were heading down the gulch and over the desert for the stamp mills in Daggett, then a heavily laden pack train, the burros being cursed and prodded by prospectors toward the back hills. When finally she was nearly run over by the local dandy taking his girl for a buggy ride, Eustacia took to the safety of the boardwalk. It, too, was crowded, the voices of Irish, Swedes, Germans, and Italians mixing together in a rich gibberish. The blacksmiths' hammers rang in quick tempo, as though engaged in a race. In the distance, the tinny toot of the narrow-gauge ore train shrilled like a tea kettle as it chugged toward the stamp mills. By the time Eustacia reached the Hurdy-Gurdy House and let herself in, escaping the crush of people, the clatter of crockery, and the foreign smells of meat-balls, rice, and goulash, her senses were exhausted.

The Hurdy-Gurdy was not open for business so early in the day. In comparison to the racket outside, it was churchlike quiet, big and dim and cool, the sun fracturing into beams through the dust. The kitchen door was open, and Eustacia headed for it. In the three days she had been in Calico, a fast friendship had grown between her and Carla—an instant comradery.

Carla sat at the small round table, her ample body draped in a purple wrapper with long, droopy sleeves. The sleeves added grace to her hands and fingers, which were curled around a plate and a serving fork. In front of her was a large platter laden with fried eggs, bacon, and cottage fried potatoes. She looked up as Eustacia stepped into the doorway. "Want some breakfast?"

"A minute ago I wasn't sure, but that looks good. Yes, please." Eustacia got an earthen mug out of the cupboard, went to the stove, and poured hot, dark coffee.

Carla chuckled. "That motley string of restaurants and boardinghouses could turn anybody's stomach."

Eustacia sat down at the table and accepted the plate of food Carla handed her. "We picked up that freighter Grant Whitman on the stage road this morning. He was bringing in his father's body. He claims Arango shot him."

Carla bent her head over her empty plate, a look of concern almost seeming to change the texture of her skin. Then she reached for the serving fork and scraped bacon and eggs onto her dish.

Eustacia, concentrating on her own food, had missed the fleeting transformation of Carla's face. Now she looked up, coffee mug in hand. "Grant believes Arango was living off his father's livestock, and when the old man discovered it and confronted him, Arango shot him down in cold blood. Grant thinks Arango is living off others, as well." Eustacia sighed. "Grant will probably be coming around to ask you questions, I'm afraid."

"Why?" Carla's voice shook a little, and she looked up abruptly from what she was doing. Unnoticed, the sleeve of her wrapper slipped up her arm.

"Because I told him you knew a lot about Calico and that perhaps you had heard something." Eustacia's reply was automatic, her eyes fastened on Carla's exposed wrist. The skin was a patchwork of deeply grooved scars, white and raised and old. Then Eustacia colored, embarrassed at her reaction—her insensitivity to Carla's feelings.

"The other wrist is exactly the same," Carla said softly. "It's all right, Eustacia, you don't have to feel—how do they say it in polite society?—so confused."

"What happened?" Eustacia couldn't help herself. Then, "If you'd rather not talk, oh, I'm sorry, Carla."

Carla smiled wryly. "We're friends. Friends want to know, maybe even need to know. It's the sharing, I guess, that brings them close together. You're the first friend I've had in a long time, Eustacia—not counting Yung Hen—and it doesn't hurt any greater to talk about the scars than when I made 'em."

Eustacia said nothing as she looked above Carla's crooked smile. The blue-gray eyes no longer seemed steely, just disappointed, and Eustacia knew she was seeing the disappointment Carla felt about her entire life.

"It's a tawdry life, being a whore. Even for those who pleasure in the occupation. Sooner or later there's ruin—disease, miscarriage, bad habits, bad men." Carla's voice was a coarse whisper on the last two words. "I've always had a talent for picking bad men."

Carla suddenly laughed. It sounded like the squawk of a parrot. Then she announced, "Some women keep making the same mistakes over and over again, and whores are no exception."

Still Eustacia said nothing. She didn't know what to say, and Carla seemed to expect nothing.

Absently, Carla picked up a piece of bacon, taking a bite. Her eyes seemed to drift far away, but the disappointment never left them. "I never liked being a whore. I reckon that's why I got into this hurdy-gurdy business, why I never take customers anymore, why I don't want to madam a house.

"I *hated* being a whore," Carla repeated, and the steel came into her jaw. "I wasn't always one, either. I was respectable once—married. He wasn't a bad man, probably only one of two I've known in my life, the second one coming right after him. But my husband was weak and not too much of a provider, and he left me a penniless widow. I fell in love again with a cowboy, soldier-of-fortune, whatever occupation was paying at the time. And, funny, he was very much like my dead husband. He had a partner . . ."

Carla's voice went hollow, as though her very being had gone numb. "He had a partner—a bad man. He waited until my cowboy was away, and then he beat and raped me. It went on for hours. I can remember afterward laying on the floor till both the wood and I got so cold that I was thanking God I'd freeze to death. Only it never really got cold enough. And then I had to do something. I guess I wasn't in my right mind, 'cause I just left everything in that place—left with what was on my back, and by then that wasn't much. I wandered into the road, and a Chinese man came along, pulling a cart. Yung Hen. He put me in his cart and took care of me—for a long time. It came to me afterward that the reason I'd run was because I knew my cowboy couldn't stand up to his partner for what had been done."

Carla swung her gaze squarely on Eustacia. It was almost businesslike. "So I had to live. When you know nothing, can't read or cipher good, and you're a woman,

57

your choices boil down to one. At first, it hardly mattered. You see, I was still numb. But it wore off, and I got sorrowful for myself. I thought, I don't have to live if I don't want to. So I slashed my wrists. I've slashed them many times, Eustacia—but someone always saves me." Her chuckle was like a small gulp. "So I guess I have to try living, after all. I think Calico is my last stop, the place I've turned over a new leaf. I'm alive. Each day's an obstacle to be challenged, battled, and, by hook or crook, beat. When it gets too rough, there's a little laudanum I keep around."

Carla smiled a little sadly, but it was a smile. "I'm still foolish about men, 'cause in the beginning I always see them for something better than they are. Probably will to the very day I die."

With Carla's sudden silence, the stillness in the Hurdy-Gurdy was even more churchlike. Embarrassed by the confidence Carla had bestowed on her, Eustacia concentrated on sipping her coffee; it was cold. She noticed Carla had begun to eat her eggs, and she knew they were cold, too. Suddenly Eustacia realized, as Carla kept her eyes on her plate, that she must be wondering if she had just lost a friend—if she had put Eustacia off with her outpouring.

Eustacia put down her coffee. "Breakfast isn't any good cold. Let's get some fresh."

Carla looked up, hope in her eyes, then relief. "Sure. Put this mess out back for the dogs."

The two women hovered over the stove, hot mugs of coffee in one hand, forks in the other pushing around eggs and bacon in frying pans. When the edges of the eggs started turning golden, Carla said, "You owe me a story, Eustacia. Remember? How you come to be in this fix, dressed like a man and all."

"I didn't start out to impersonate a boy. It just seemed that the clothes would make the journey across the Mojave from San Bernardino easier. San Bernardino is where we live."

"We?"

"My husband and two daughters."

"What are *you* doing here, then?"

"Looking for my husband. Have you ever heard of Philip Kibbe, Carla?" There was a note of desperation in Eustacia's voice.

Carla thought a moment, then sighed. "I'd like to be able to say yes, hon. But never, and you gotta admit that's not a John Smith name. It's a name folks would remember. But go on and tell your story. Maybe I can think of a way to help."

"Philip and I have been married sixteen years, and they've been fairly happy ones. He's really very special, Carla, gallant and caring and gentle. So it hardly mattered he's been involved in many failed enterprises in San Bernardino. One person can't be everything. We always managed to get by until he got something else. He was never bitter when a position didn't work out. And I was luckier than you in terms of education. My father saw to it that I had the best available, which wasn't difficult, because we were army and there always was a post school. So when Philip was between enterprises—which was often, I'm afraid—I could always find some piecework—clerking, bookkeeping.

"Anyway, this last time, Philip decided he'd come up here to Calico and see if he could develop a silver strike. Carla, that was six months ago, and nary a word since. That's not like Philip. I'm so afraid—I guess, that I might find out he's dead—but I have to know. I have to know that, or know what's gone terribly wrong."

It was as though Eustacia, once started, couldn't stop: "So I left the girls with my father in San Bernardino and came up here. When things worked out the way they did about my mistaken identity, I jumped at the open stage job, since I realized that finding Philip may take time—and my savings won't last long."

"Going to be some red faces if you're ever found out, Eustacia—the men's, not yours!" Carla chuckled. "You say you got two girls?"

"Ophelia and Collette. Collette is my baby. She's only six. Ophelia is fifteen. She's going to be a beautiful woman. She's so much like Philip, and the two are very attached. This has all been very hard on her." Eustacia sighed. "Now I don't know how I'm going to find her father. I didn't expect him to be standing on a Calico street corner waiting for me, but neither did I expect there wouldn't be the faintest trace. I just don't know where to look next, Carla."

"Now, dear, you've hardly scraped the surface. There's lots of places he could be in these hills. Bismarck, for one." Carla whipped her pan off the flame. "Come on, let's just swap some of the contents and eat out of the pans." She flipped an egg into Eustacia's frying pan, fishing out strips of bacon for herself.

"Where's Bismarck?"

"Silver camp over the ridge. Nothing like this. In fact, the Bismarck kids come over here to school."

"How do I get there?"

"Well, if you hurry up your eating and go see James Stacy, the postmaster, you can walk over with the mail."

Eustacia gulped down her breakfast and then headed out of the kitchen. "I'll see you later."

"It might be after opening time, Eustacia. I have to look in on some property of mine outside of Calico. And another thing, while I love having you stay here, the Hurdy-Gurdy really isn't fitting accommodations— especially if you ever need to get to bed early. So I've made arrangements for you to stay at Yung Hen's." Then to Eustacia's unspoken question, Carla said, "Yes, he knows. He had to make proper arrangements. But you're safe. Yung Hen's sworn to silence. Now get on with you."

On her way to James Stacy's, Eustacia checked in at Mojave Station. The place seemed deserted except for Harv Miller, who was washing down the stage. Despite Frank Eberson's warning and her own belief that she ought to leave well enough alone, Eustacia was still curious about Grant Whitman. The vague thought was forming in the back of her mind that, in the long run, she would be safer if she knew as much about everyone as possible. Maybe that was just an excuse.

"Harv," Eustacia broached, "have you been in this part of the Mojave long?"

"Goodly piece."

"As long as the Whitmans?"

"Sure. Used to work as an extra hand for Reynold now and again. A sorry thing to see Grant bring him in that way this morning."

"What do you know about Grant?" Eustacia was surprised at her bluntness.

However, if Harv Miller was disturbed by the boy Stash's interest, he didn't show it. Perhaps he just welcomed the companionship, and since there was no harm in such talk, he never gave the whole situation a thought.

Slowly, Harv kept sponging at the wheel with his rag. "Well now, he was a good boy, and he grew into a fine man. He was always befriending the underdog and looking out for children and such. Likes them a lot. He likes women, too, not just in the way most men do, but for their company—what they have to say and their interests. Maybe that comes from losing his mother so young. Kind of gave him a natural curiosity."

Harv tossed the rag into his bucket and sloshed it around to rinse it out. "His daddy was real proud of

61

him when he joined up with the army. Grant always had a strong sense of duty and a need to finish everything he started. That seemed to serve him in good stead in the army. Reynold said he had a bang-up career going. That's kinda what surprised me about him coming back here to drive freight. Wonder what happened."

As Eustacia drifted away, leaving the old man to his thoughts, she was thinking that perhaps nothing had happened to Grant's army career. As an army child, she had seen men draw stranger assignments. Who or what was he after, then? Arango? Something to do with Calico's silver production? Or maybe he was really what he seemed—a man who had tired of the army and had come home.

When Eustacia reached the postmaster's cabin, James Stacy was strapping the leather mail pouches to his dog Dorsey's back. The dog was a black and white shepherd with a black back and white chest and legs, his face marked like a mask by the two colors. His ears were floppy, his tail bushy. He stood perfectly still, almost as if he realized the importance of his job.

"Mr. Stacy?"

James Stacy looked up. "What can I do for you, boy?"

"I need to get to Bismarck, and since I'm new in the area, I don't rightly know the way. Could I walk along with you and your dog?"

"Stash, ain't it, the boy stage driver?"

"Yes, sir."

"You're polite enough, I'll say that. Sure, you can go along, but I'm not going. Just Dorsey." Seeing Eustacia's look of surprise, he added, "Don't worry, Dorsey knows the way real good, and he'll be glad to show you. But mark your trail so if you don't come back together, you won't get lost in the hills."

"Thank you. But how did you train a dog to carry the mail?"

James Stacy straightened up and laughed. "Lord, that's a story now. Of course you got to start with a naturally smart dog, which Dorsey is." He patted the shepherd's head. "Back in '83, I opened my door one morning to find this dog sitting outside. Lord knows where he came from, except he was real footsore and hungry. I'd say he'd been traveling awhile. Anyway, I doctored him and fed him and kind of let him adopt me. Now, I got mining interests in Bismarck, and me and my partner go back and forth over the three miles real regular-like. Well, Dorsey would come along. He got friendly with my partner and took to spending some of his time with him, sharing the two cabins, so to speak.

"One day I had to get a hold of my partner real quick. So I wrote out a note, rolled it in a bandanna, and tied it around the dog's neck. Then I pointed him toward Bismarck and told him to find my partner. What really surprised me was that he not only connected with my partner, but he brought back an answer to my note. So we started communicating like that regularly. Certainly saved us the three-mile trek. Then it came to me that if the dog could carry our notes, why couldn't he carry the mail? So I tried him, and he did fine. That's when I took to calling him Dorsey, after the postmaster before me."

Eustacia shook her head. "That's quite a story, Mr. Stacy. He looks so settled and serious."

"That's because Dorsey knows this is important business. But you watch what happens when those mail pouches come off. He'll be barking and jumping and wagging that big fluff tail of his, making the rounds of all his Bismarck friends to see who's saved him a biscuit or piece of fat. Same thing when he gets back here with his load." He turned to the shepherd. "All right, Dorsey, get to work, and mind the boy here."

The dog cocked his head at Eustacia, then started across the ridge at a trot, Eustacia trailing after him.

Grant found the front door of the Hurdy-Gurdy House open and went inside. Across the barnlike room, he saw Carla coming through the doorway behind the bar, her hands tucked across her chest into the deep sleeves of her purple wrapper. She seemed deep in thought, jumping a little when she realized he was in the room.

"Not open yet," she called.

Grant closed the distance, catching her at the end of the bar. "I know, Carla, but I need some help. Stash said you know a lot about Calico, and I need some information. Arango killed my father this morning."

A look of weariness passed over Carla's face. "I'm sorry about your pa, but I'm sure I don't know any more about Arango than the rest of the town."

"I didn't mean it like that. You talk to a lot of people, overhear a lot of conversations in this place. Carla, have you ever heard anyone complaining about losing a lot of stock—" Grant took a deep breath "—just like Arango and his bunch were living off my father's spread?"

"So that's how you think Arango's making it on the Mojave. He was living off your father?"

Carla didn't stop for an answer, and Grant guessed she knew everything about this morning from Eustacia.

"So you've got a vendetta going now, and you expect to catch up with Arango by searching out the ranchers who seem to be having trouble. Let me tell you something, Grant. If anyone had a mind to complain—and I've never heard a word—after today they wouldn't. If Arango shot your pa, the example's been set. If he's taken to killing unwilling hosts, a person would certainly be safer to ignore his presence and let him stay. In silence."

Carla moved around Grant, patting his arm. "I really am sorry. Now I've got to get dressed."

As Grant left the Hurdy-Gurdy, he had to admit Carla was right. His search for the Mexican bandit was going to be even more difficult now. There would be a conspiracy of silence among the ranchers. Moreover, the Calico Mountains were honeycombed with mines and tunnels, good places to hide for short periods.

Suddenly Grant thought it wouldn't hurt to talk to the miners. Perhaps someone had seen something. He would begin with Bismarck and eventually work his way to Borate and the borax mines. Perhaps some of the twenty-mule-team drivers had caught a glimpse of Arango during their long crossings over the Mojave.

Grant went back to Delameter's freight company, picked up his horse, and headed toward Bismarck. On the way Dorsey, the mail dog, passed him on his return trip home.

Bismarck was much smaller and rougher than Calico, but it still had its share of saloons and a merchandising store. Grant decided to try the saloons first, and it didn't take more than two before Grant realized he was following behind someone who was also inquiring about strangers. Curious, Grant skipped the next couple of saloons in the row, moving on to what appeared to be the latest establishment. It was merely a large tent, the bar a board resting on beer kegs, the bottles of whiskey pulled from wooden boxes behind the bar. Glancing through the flap into the dimness, Grant saw Stash talking to the bartender. He got a queer feeling in his stomach, almost wished it hadn't been the woman, Eustacia Kibbe, he'd been following. Suddenly he realized he wanted to like her, but he was afraid that whatever she was up to was going to prevent that. But the situation was upon him now. He had to know what her business was and whether it was remotely connected to Arango and whoever his contacts were on the Mojave.

So Grant set an ambush. He passed the tent saloon and continued toward the merchandising store. There was a break of cleared ground between the saloons and the store, occupied by a haphazardly thrown together woodpile. He ducked along the side and waited.

Obligingly, Eustacia came along a few minutes later. Grant's hand snaked out and clasped her forearm, swinging her body to face him. Momentarily, her face turned the color of a blanched almond, then pink slowly began crawling up her neck. She was angry, and he knew he had given her a bad turn, pouncing on her like that. He had hoped the ploy would rattle some answers out of her, but she was recovering fast.

Eustacia shook Grant's hand away. "Do you normally waylay young men like this? You can't be bothered with just walking up to someone you know and saying 'howdy' civilized-like?"

Somehow Grant felt like he was on the defensive already. He tried to regain the initiative. "Who'd think I'd be trailing the Calico stage driver who's asking questions all over town about strangers?"

"You knew!" Eustacia did not know if he did or not, but her father had taught her the best defense was a strong offense. "And if you know I've been asking questions, then you've been asking them, too! Who are you looking for, Grant, and why? What's your business, Mr. Freightdriver?"

Grant didn't want to fight with Eustacia Kibbe. What he really wanted to do was to get to know her better and discover why it was so necessary for her to pose as a boy. "Let's call a truce, Stash. We haven't had trouble before. In fact, we've always been on the same side. Most likely, we still are."

Grant watched Eustacia's jaw and head bridle as she worked to calm herself. Then the pink began fading from her neck.

"All right, Grant." Eustacia sounded a little tired. "What are you doing here? Looking for Arango? Someone who's seen him perhaps, or whoever his arm is out of the Mojave?"

"After this morning, don't you think I have a pretty good reason?"

"That's it, then." It was a statement, but the words held an underlying question. Eustacia thought about mentioning his army connection, then held back. They were not ready for total confidences. This confrontation was like a preliminary probe.

"Carla wasn't much help this morning," Grant went on, "except that she made a lot of sense when she said the ranchers wouldn't betray Arango now. So it means stumbling around out here until I find something. Obviously, you're in the same boat, Stash. Who are you looking for?"

Eustacia didn't miss a beat. "My brother, Philip Kibbe. He came out here six months ago to mine silver, and I've had nary a word since."

Grant was thinking that it had been in the last six months that Arango had come north. Her brother was probably a pile of bones somewhere on the Mojave if his trail had crossed Arango's, but he did not want to tell Eustacia that. Let her look for him. Perhaps she would find him alive and well, just a little careless with paper and pencil. If she did not, then she would eventually give up and go away without knowing the horrible truth. There would always be hope. In either case, Eustacia Kibbe would stay around the Mojave for a while, and that was what Grant selfishly wanted.

Eustacia glanced up at the sky, gauging the time of day by the sun. "Well," she sighed, "that's all of my questions for the day. I've got to get back to Calico. There's the afternoon stage run." She stepped away from the woodpile, then glanced back at Grant. "If you're curious, I've had no sign of Philip—and nothing on Arango." She squared her shoulders and walked toward the ridge.

Grant watched Eustacia until she disappeared. Then he went back to the tent bar and ordered a beer.

After Carla had watched Grant walk out of the Hurdy-Gurdy and into the street from an upstairs window, she dressed slowly. She was really in no hurry to get to her business. It had been a depressing morning, a morning during which she had felt continually off balance. Dread at what she would find at her small Mojave ranch had begun to grow in her, beginning with Eustacia's news about Reynold. When she got into the rented buggy, the worry increased with each mile that crawled away, and when Carla finally reached her place, her suspicions were confirmed. Arango's men were in the yard, as she had known all along they would be— even while she was denying everything to Eustacia and Grant.

Carla sat for a moment, her hands folded in her lap, and tried to figure out how she had got herself into such a mess. Many of the things she had told Eustacia were true—even the part about making a conscious decision to live, to improve the quality of her life. But what she said and did varied considerably. It seemed each time she made a positive move, she had to do something destructive to herself, almost as if to negate her self-worth. Arango was the latest.

She had been harboring him and sleeping with him on and off since his arrival in the Mojave. She supposed she had been taken in at the beginning by his fine rhetoric about helping the oppressed people of Mexico. But it hadn't taken her long to see it for the sham it was. Still, she did not extract herself from the situation, even when she realized he was probably the worst of the lot of men she had had, even when he physically abused her. Now she was afraid. If Arango had killed Reynold simply because the old man had annoyed him, then she was really out of her league.

There was no further point in putting it off. Marshaling her fear, Carla got out of the buggy and walked slowly to the house. Arango was there with the good-looking American, Emil. Arango sat with his booted feet up on a table, smoking. He barely acknowledged Carla when she came in, seeming to be lost in thought. She could not tell if he and Emil had been talking.

Carla stayed near the door, her shoulder almost brushing the doorjamb. "Francisco," she said, "did you kill Reynold Whitman early this morning?"

Arango looked at her, his eyes hard and hawklike, his voice soft and cheerful. "My dear, I killed an old man who objected to me slaughtering a few cows to feed my hungry *amigos*. If that was this Whitman, then yes. He was nothing, an annoyance. Better off gone, that one." Then he deliberately looked away from her, dismissing her. Moving one foot back and forth, he methodically began carving a groove into the table surface with his spur.

Carla watched, shocked, flinching as though the steel was biting across her face.

Suddenly from outside came horrible screeching, the clang of kicked tin pails, and ribald laughter. Carla swung around and pulled the door open. Feathers blew into her face, down sticking to her moist lips. Her stomach turned over as she saw what was happening. Arango's men had turned her chickens out into the yard and were savagely making sport. Several were pinned to the ground, knives through their bodies, flapping and struggling as they slowly bled to death. Some had legs or wings torn off. Others were being thrown back and forth in a bizarre game of catch. Everywhere there were blood and feathers and running fowls.

Spinning back into the room, her hand on her forehead, her eyes half closed, Carla cried, "Make them stop! Francisco, make them stop! Please!"

Arango laughed, never budging from his chair. "*Mis amigos* desire *pollo* for supper, Carla, and you have never denied me—or anyone else, for that matter—anything before."

The revulsion came on the wave of bile that pushed up her throat. It was a revulsion that would never go away. She could feel it contorting her face. Quickly she tried to relax her features, but she knew by the quick look that darted through Arango's eyes that she had not succeeded. Without a word, Carla turned and walked out of her house through the blood and feathers to the buggy. With shaking hands she gathered up the reins and started back to Calico.

"Perhaps, Francisco, you should not have been so harsh with her," Philip commented quietly. "She knows a great deal about us and the movement."

"*Sí*, I saw her look. She is done with me. It could not be lost on even such a stupid whore that there was no need for the chickens with so much of the rancher's beef fresh killed. Ah, so like the chickens, her neck must be wrung!"

"But she might still be useful," Philip suggested.

Arango contemplated that thought. Then with a wave of his hand, almost imperial, he said, "Perhaps you are right, Emil. For the present, oil should be poured on troubled waters. You will do the pouring, *mi amigo inglés*. Pour yourself into her. You should have no trouble. I have seen the great calf eyes she has for you lately. Go to the whore and bed her—*for the cause!* When he said the last, he had to turn his head away so Philip wouldn't see him smirking.

Philip hesitated a moment, seemed about to speak, then strode out of the house. He found his horse and started after the buggy. His obedience was not entirely altruistic. It had been six months since he had had a woman, since he had left Eustacia.

It wasn't long before he caught up with her. He pulled alongside, grabbing the reins and halting the buggy.

Carla looked at him. "Did Francisco send you, Emil, to wring my neck, too?" Her voice was acid.

Although Philip disliked criticizing Arango, he often thought Francisco was too quick to underestimate people. Carla Maxey was not a stupid woman, as her last statement proved. But she could be swayed. She needed a little romance in her life, just as he did.

Philip cleared his throat. "No, but we need to talk—as one friend to another. These are troubled times. You will be my friend, Carla?"

Carla looked up into his blue eyes and curly, golden blond hair, and she was lost. She knew she was going to be a victim again. For the moment, she did not care.

Chapter Six

It was midday by the time Eustacia traipsed back over the ridge into Calico. She was discouraged, hot, thirsty, and hungry after the six-mile round trip. Yet underneath all that was the same determined feeling that had made her square her shoulders when walking away from Grant. Although she had discovered nothing in Bismarck, she was intent on continuing her search for Philip. Suddenly it occurred to her that she could be in Calico a long time.

Eustacia gained Wall Street, her discouragement slipping toward depression. She missed her children, even as sharp as Ophelia could be with her tongue. She missed little Collette's soft touch on her arm and the way she wiggled onto her lap. She realized that the girls were safe and well off in her father's care. And they knew where she was, because she had wired them almost immediately. So it was not that she and the girls were lost to each other—as Philip was to them. Yet the separation cut keenly through Eustacia like a cold wind.

Relentlessly, Eustacia pushed her yearning for her

family to the back of her mind. She could not afford the luxury of self-pity.

She marched herself to the Hurdy-Gurdy House but found the place soundly locked. Then she remembered Carla had said she was going to check some property or other and probably wouldn't be back until opening time. Sighing, Eustacia turned around and stared next door at Yung Hen's boardinghouse. Well, there was no time like the present to see her new accommodations.

Shambling, Eustacia entered the dim front hallway. Heavy tassles screened the top half of the entrances to two large rooms, one on either side of her. One was probably the dining room, the other a parlor. Down the long hallway, from the very back of the boardinghouse, she heard the clanking of pans and the rapid-fire, short-syllable sound of Chinese. The kitchen, no doubt. In front of her rose a boxy stairwell leading to the boarders' rooms.

Suddenly Yung Hen was beside her, his fingertips barely brushing her sleeve. Eustacia had not heard him. She looked at his feet; they were slippered. He had probably come from the dining room. His eyes darted over her with birdlike sharpness, no doubt judging her disguise.

"I want to thank you and your friends for helping when the town was ready to hang me," Yung Hen said in a precise, unaccented English, with no *l*'s sliding in for *r*'s. He smiled at her surprise. "I am educated. There was a mission school in my province. With practice and a good teacher, Chinese can overcome the *r*, though it puts the devil on the tongue."

"Carla says she told you everything, Yung Hen."

"My mind knows, but my mouth has no words, Mrs. Kibbe. It was necessary. You see, many of the men sleep together. In the larger rooms, sometimes eight. That would not do for you, obviously. I have put you in a safe place—quiet, all to itself. It is in the back and looks to the mountains."

"Thank you, Yung Hen. Carla is very good to look out for me—and you are, too."

"Carla is a good woman." Yung Hen paused, then added cryptically, "But she is often foolish, and now she walks with danger." He began up the stairs. "Come, I will show you now. You are tired and hungry."

As Eustacia followed Yung Hen, she wondered dully what more there was to Carla that she didn't know. Suddenly the depression she'd been fending off since her return from Bismarck swamped her, dunking her in icy uncertainty as surely as if she were a sinking boat in the Mojave River. Everything and everybody seemed not to be what they were—Carla, Grant, especially herself.

After Yung Hen deposited her at a doorway with a bob of his head, Eustacia surveyed her new accommodations. The room was clean and light, with an iron bedstead and cheap wooden furniture—more than adequate. She moved to the basin and pitcher and found that Yung Hen had already provided water. She poured it into the basin and discovered the water was warm and lightly scented with lemon. Grateful for the consideration, Eustacia washed her face and hands, then lay down on the bed, wiggling her boots off by pushing one against the other. All of a sudden she realized how tired and achy her arms and back were, as though those parts of her body were held together by knotted cords. She smiled ironically. Driving the stage had done that to her. Momentarily her forehead puckered. She had been several days on the job, and William Curry had still said nothing about making her permanent. In fact, he'd had little or nothing to say at all. He just watched.

There was a light tap on the thin wooden door

panels. Eustacia pushed herself off the bed and padded across the plank floor in her thickly socked feet. When she opened the door, a Chinese man stood there, holding a tray of food. The man bowed slightly, offering the tray. Eustacia took it. "Thank you," she said, but the man's footsteps were already a whisper in the hallway.

Eustacia carried the tray to the bureau and set it down. There was a bowl of clear broth, probably chicken, with bits of meat and Chinese cabbage in it, a bowl of rice laced with the same, hot fragrant tea, and some other drink that Eustacia, after tasting its potent tartness, thought might be rice wine. It dulled the ache of her body and of her heart, and as she spooned the soup into herself, she suddenly realized that was why she had gone straight to the Hurdy-Gurdy House after returning from Bismarck. She had wanted a drink of spirits. After only a week of searching in this place, she was already going to the dogs.

Eustacia ate and drank everything and felt better for it. Then she pulled her boots back on and let herself out of her room. The boardinghouse seemed as quiet and empty as when she had arrived, although she was sure some of the boarders had been to the dining room. She glanced in as she passed and saw two Chinese clearing. She did not see Yung Hen.

Out on Wall Street, she headed toward Mojave Station. It still was warm, but she fancied a chill in the breeze that perked up every so often. When she got to the station, the stage was already pulled out front, hitched, and pointed back down Wall Street for Daggett. Harv Miller and Frank Eberson stood beside it. When they saw Stash coming, they started snickering. Eustacia, apprehensive at their reaction, tried to shy away.

Eberson called out, "Hey, Stash, old boy, what's with all this special treatment the Chinaman be givin' you? Got your own private digs and a tray sent up.

Course by the looks of the stuff, I wouldn't eat it. Give me a chop and mashed taters and gravy any old time. That's what we common folk had downstairs. See, Harv and me room at Yung Hen's, too."

Eustacia remained silent, but she could feel the warm pink beginning to creep up her throat.

Harv Miller chuckled softly. "Look, Frank, the lad's blushing. Ain't seen a boy do that in a coon's age. Least ways not after his first time." He turned back to Eustacia. "Now what's a young 'un like you got going, Stash? You got the Hurdy-Gurdy woman in your pocket and now the Chinaman. Course, it's common knowledge Yung Hen and Carla are friends—maybe more."

"Now," cautioned Eberson, "I wouldn't be spreadin' that too much around, Harv, 'cause folks feel funny about a white woman bein' with a yellow man. There's even a law in California against the two marryin'. Did you know that, Stash?"

Eustacia nodded, wishing she could drop through the ground.

"I'm only talking among us three friends," Miller said, and then his voice dropped to a licentious whisper as he continued, "What I want to know is, do you got something going with both of them, Stash? All three of you at the same time!"

Eustacia was shocked, and she felt like every part of her body was glowing red.

"Looks like a regular Fourth of July rocket, don't he!" Miller cackled.

But even Frank Eberson seemed uncomfortable with the turn the ribbing had taken. "Ah, leave off now, Harv."

Miller was about to goad the point, but just then a deep voice called out from behind him, "Get back to work, Harv." Miller spun around to see William Curry standing in the doorway of Mojave Station. He didn't look angry, just bored.

Harv Miller's eyes dropped to the ground. Curry chose to ignore the situation and just continued talking as though he had heard nothing. "I've an announcement, and Stash here probably thinks it's been a long time coming. Stash has been driving several days now without mishap, so I've decided he's hired permanent. Congratulations, Stash. Now all of you move your tails, or my stage is going to be late into Daggett."

There were no passengers for the trip out. Relieved by both Curry's decision and the end of the men's teasing, Eustacia scrambled up on the box and grabbed the reins and, as soon as Eberson was on board, smartly cracked the whip and started the team down Wall Street.

Eustacia was silent on the way out of town. She was angry and embarrassed at the things that had been said. That she, even as a married woman, had had to hear such insinuations was preposterous! Then she pulled herself up short, her sense of irony asserting itself. Neither Eberson nor Harv Miller knew her true identity. As Eustacia realized, society dictated that they never would have had such sport, even among themselves, in the presence of a lady. She supposed what she had just experienced was the way men hazed each other.

Suddenly Eustacia felt as if she had been living under a rock most of her life. She wondered if Philip acted like Eberson and Miller when he was not with her. It was hard to imagine Philip behaving that way. Perhaps not all men behaved as the roustabout and the express messenger. Then suddenly, unbidden, Eustacia wondered about Grant. Flustered by her silent question, she cracked the whip and set the horses into their collars.

* * *

The San Bernardino stage was pounding away its last lap toward Daggett. Inside, Ophelia Kibbe thought her bones would surely shatter. Across the aisle, her sister, Collette, was enjoying the rough ride with all the unbridled enthusiasm of an adventurous six year old. *The little heathen,* Ophelia thought disgustedly.

It was not that Ophelia disliked her sister. She loved her with all her heart, and there had been lots of fun between them when Collette had been a baby and a toddler. But now the gap between their ages seemed so great. Ophelia told herself the problem was that she had the interests and perceptions of a woman, while Collette was, as must be expected, only a child.

Ophelia was not shy about feeling superior. In truth, there was some basis for the feeling. Like her father, her hair was blond, her eyes the color of bluebells. She was slender and moved like a reed swaying lightly in the marsh breeze. On the less positive side, at fifteen she was so preoccupied with becoming a proper lady that she was prissy. She thought of her father in the most idealistic terms and was fiercely loyal to him. And that was why, when she was not worrying about her manners or her dress—especially alone at night—she admitted to the ache that came from everywhere inside her, to the confusion and fear she felt with her father's disappearance.

Collette was almost as attractive as her sister, but in a different way. Her hair was walnut colored, her eyes brown, her eyelashes thick and black. She felt closer to her mother, partly because of her age, partly because, being a more pragmatic child, Collette had early discovered she could not compete with her sister for her father's affection. As a result, her feelings for him were far less intense.

Collette looked across at her sister and saw the pinched look on Ophelia's face that always meant she was holding herself rigid against something—in this case, the bumpy ride. "Gosh, Ophelia, won't it be grand to see Mama again!"

"Yes, of course, Collette. I just hope she's found Daddy, and we can all turn around and get out of that provincial little town and back to San Bernardino. Absent young ladies don't get their dance cards filled or get invited to the fine holiday outings that are sure to be coming. Besides, what could be proper about a silver camp named Calico! At least the founding fathers could have named it something Spanish and romantic."

Collette was bored and a little overwhelmed by her sister's rattling on, so her voice sounded small. "Well, it sounds fun to me. Besides, Grandpa couldn't help he got sick, too sick for us to take care of him. Mrs. Sherman was just trying to do the best for all of us by sending us to Mama while she takes care of Grandpa."

"Just like you, Collette, to see it from a child's view of adventure. But then, little dear, you have no choice just yet. Wait till you get older. You'll see things differently."

"I hope not as stupid as you," Collette muttered.

"Now, let's not wrangle anymore. It looks like this stupid contraption is finally going to stop."

"This is only Daggett. There'll be another stage to where Mama is."

Ophelia's face, which had momentarily brightened, fell. "Well, at least this stop will allow my bones to stop clacking together."

The San Bernardino stage lurched to a halt in choking dust and various degrees of whiplash. When the dust had cleared, Collette pointed eagerly out the window. "See, there it is, Ophelia. It's even red!"

Ophelia glanced at the other stagecoach, saw three men gathered near it, and prepared to alight. She was determined not to give the next leg of their journey another thought. It was something that just had to be endured.

Eustacia was standing with Eberson and Luke Portage, half listening to them quarrel, when the San Bernardino coach pulled into Daggett Station. She always hoped some pearl of information about Philip would drop from either of them as they argued over every bit of news in the area. So far she would have had more luck finding a pearl in the mud.

Eustacia moved a little away from the men as the San Bernardino passengers began to alight. Suddenly her stomach fell into her abdomen and hung there swaying, it seemed, by threads. "God preserve us all!"

Collette, who had managed to get off the stage before her sister, was winding her way like a regular street urchin through the other bustling passengers, intent on the corral and barn area. In San Bernardino, there had been no such exploring. Mrs. Sherman had held her hand tightly at the station, Ophelia standing stoically on her other side, until it had been time to board. Now she was going to see all about how stages worked.

Too late, Ophelia saw her sister's vanishing back in the crowd. Swiftly, she broke into a trot, thinking how undignified she must look. *I may still wring the little begger's neck!* she thought grimly.

Eustacia swung around the Mojave Station coach to the side away from Eberson and Portage and, skirting around the station house, moved to intercept Collette. Her brain kept pounding, *What are they doing here? How am I going to deal with this?*

Eustacia tapped Collette on her jacketed shoulder. She noticed it was her brown winter jacket. The little girl swung her head up, got a quick impression of a hat, and concentrated back on the corral of horses she had been studying, her arms crossed on the top rail, her feet balanced on another.

"Collette, don't you know your own mama?" Eustacia whispered.

Birdlike, the small face turned up again, and then her mouth began to open. She released the top rail and would have fallen had Eustacia not grabbed her shoulders.

"Shh, dear, not a word," Eustacia cautioned. "I'll explain."

"Mother?" Ophelia was incredulous. She had come upon the pair soon enough to overhear the short exchange.

"Ophelia, darling, it's quite a story."

"I'm sure it is. But what are you doing dressed like—*that!*"

"I drive the stage between Calico and Daggett."

"You what? Oh, Mother."

"Now, Ophelia, everything will make sense in a bit."

"Everyone thinks you're a man, don't they?"

"Yes, Ophelia."

"Oh, Mother, no."

"Ophelia, get hold of yourself. You have not yet suffered a social disaster." Eustacia's lips turned up at the corners, her eyes crinkling.

"Mama, this is exciting!" Collette declared. "Will you teach me all about the stage? Can we take special rides? Oh, Mama, you're the best!"

"I know, but you have to keep this all a secret, Collette. Not a word, little one!" Eustacia said firmly.

The little girl's face fell, almost as if she had discovered on Christmas morning that St. Nick had forgotten to fill her stocking. Slowly, she nodded.

"Ophelia?"

The older girl's gesture was decisive, as if saying, *I would just die if anyone knew my mother dressed as a man and drove a stage*.

"Now, what are you two doing here?"

"Grandpa got real sick, Mama," Collette volunteered.

Eustacia shot a questioning look at Ophelia.

"That's right, Mother. No one's sure with what, but Mrs. Sherman is nursing him. She shipped us off here to you." Ophelia had the grace to look embarrassed at her last words.

"Well, we'll have to make the best of it." Eustacia hid the worry in her matter-of-factness. "Now, listen to me, both of you. I am your uncle looking for your father. If anyone asks you questions, don't say any more than that. Understand?"

"Yes, Mother."

"Yes, Mama."

"Come along, then. The stage should be leaving." With an arm around Collette's shoulders, Eustacia turned back toward the station house. She heard Ophelia fall in step behind them.

Before the three reached the coach, Ophelia's voice came little and soft out of the gathering dusk and chill. "Mother, any news about Daddy?"

"No, not yet."

After that, the girls were silent—all the way into Calico, staring as the bands of color on the mountains turned purple, then black. The girls seemed deflated, whether from the unexpected meeting with their mother, the mention of their father, or the simple letdown and weariness of a long journey.

In the distance, as the stage rolled toward Wall Street, Eustacia glimpsed the cemetery. People were trailing down the slope from it. Reynold Whitman's funeral apparently was over. For a second longer, Eustacia could see Grant standing over the grave, a silhouette, and then the stage was rushing past into the early evening confusion of Calico.

Eustacia drove mechanically, her thoughts with Grant. Suddenly she felt as hollow and sore inside as he must. It surprised her. She had not known his father and did not even know Grant well. Yet, the feeling, the loss, the unsettledness was there. Perhaps she felt so intensely because her own father was ill and her husband was missing. Perhaps it was the complication her children's arrival created. But whatever the reason, there was an achy lump in her throat that would not swallow away.

Eustacia kicked on the brake in front of Mojave Station and jumped from the box, swinging open the stage door. She lifted Collette out, then helped Ophelia. Ophelia, reading the silent message in her mother's eyes, grasped her sister's hand and said, "We'll just wait quietly here." Collette nodded tiredly.

By the time Eustacia got around to the rear boot, Harv Miller and Frank Eberson had the luggage out in a neat half circle. Eustacia swung up two carpetbags, muttered a good night at the two men, then nodded at the girls. They fell in step behind, and the three began threading their way down Wall Street to Yung Hen's.

Eberson shook his head, mumbling, "Wonder what gives now?"

Harv Miller shrugged. After this afternoon, he was less interested in Stash's business.

Eustacia and her children looked neither to the left nor to the right, so tired in body and spirit were they. Yung Hen's sign, waving slowly in the cool wind, meant an oasis, a refuge, a place to collect themselves and their thoughts. So none of them saw Grant Whitman stop on the other side of the Hurdy-Gurdy House and stare speculatively as they entered the boardinghouse.

Fresh from the cemetery, his sorrow and anger a gnawing gut ache, Grant was looking for anything to distract him. Seeing Eustacia with two children was a

83

sure draw. People shouldered around him as he stood still on the boardwalk long after the trio had disappeared. Most, no doubt, attributed his action to grief, and they tacitly left him alone.

Suddenly Grant gathered himself and remembered to walk. He continued past the Hurdy-Gurdy and Yung Hen's and entered the Globe Restaurant instead. He had heard they had steaks tonight, brought up by freighter that afternoon from Daggett.

As he sat down at a table and took the offered coffee, his mind abruptly cleared. It was as though someone had laid the picture, bright and clear, in front of him. Eustacia was not looking for her brother, but for her husband. Moreover, she had two children to support. She had found a way of doing it with the quickest method at hand—fighting for and winning the Calico stage driver's job. Grant had nothing but admiration for her; he liked practicality in a woman. Then a smile quirked his lips. He was also amused by her guile, though that would not have seen her through if she had not had the skill with the stage reins.

Grant leaned back in his chair, the thought opening new areas of intrigue. What kind of life had Eustacia had to give her such skill with horse teams? What kind of a man was she married to? Was she looking for him out of duty or love? Had he left her, or as she had indicated, had he mysteriously disappeared, perhaps even been murdered?

The platter of steak came, the waitress clattering the crockery down in front of him. Grant glanced at it, the meat hot and juicy, the string beans steaming in a bowl, and he was suddenly no longer interested in eating. It was not the food. It was just that in solving part of the mystery about Eustacia Kibbe, he had discovered another. Yet his reaction was different this time. It was not just curiosity that moved him now.

Gone was the hesitancy he had felt earlier in the day when they were in Bismarck. Perhaps seeing her with the children had made the difference. Something reached out to him now—a very determined lady trying to go it alone.

Grant clamped off the thought. Embarrassed at himself, he picked up his knife and fork and began cutting his steak. Here he was again butting into business that didn't concern him. Eustacia might not even want his help. Grant took a determined bite. Well, she was going to get it anyway. As long as he was asking questions about Arango, he could ask a few unrelated ones about Eustacia's husband.

Eustacia softly closed the door to the adjoining room in Yung Hen's boardinghouse. She turned around and wearily crossed her room. On the bureau there was a sip or two of the rice wine left from dinner. She took the small, cream-colored earthen cup and sat down on the edge of the bed.

She had not stopped moving since arriving at Yung Hen's with her family. Graciously he had provided the extra room, a tin tub of hot water, and trays of food from the kitchen. Ophelia had taken care of her own needs, but Collette was so tired that Eustacia had had to help her. She had bathed Collette and shampooed the dust out of her hair, plaiting it in a thick braid down her back, then dressed her in her soft flannel gown. She had had to force her six-year-old to eat, though Yung Hen had seen to it that the food was easily digestible—a hash topped with a poached egg. The last problem had been getting both girls to drink the Chinese tea. Now Eustacia figured the struggle had been worth it, because almost immediately afterward Ophelia and Collette had fallen asleep.

Eustacia sighed. There were so many extra complications now, not to mention the nagging worry about her father. What could have made him so ill that the girls had to be sent away? She decided that first thing in the morning she would telegraph San Bernardino.

She took a sip of her wine, her mind flicking back over the day. She was beginning to wish she had some help in her undertaking. The very size of the Mojave she would have to search was overwhelming. Then, too, as strong as she was and as capable as she had always been, she was realizing this challenge was bigger than anything she had had to deal with in her life. Perhaps she couldn't do it all by herself. She needed some shoring up, and she thought of Grant, not Carla.

Then Eustacia had doubts. Why had she thought of Grant before Carla? Was it because, since time began, women were taught to look to men for help and protection? She knew first hand that it was not always provided. Was it because Carla seemed to be having a hard struggle of her own? Or was it just the realization that Grant would be in a better position to get results?

The questions were tiring Eustacia out more than all the physical exertion of the day. But as long as she was asking questions, she might as well be asking them to miners in the Hurdy-Gurdy House. She roused herself, slipped from her room, and went next door to Carla's place, as she had done every night since her arrival. She asked everyone new about Philip, but this night was the same as all the others. No one knew anything.

Worn down, Eustacia finally glanced around for Carla. She saw her coming out of the kitchen, food on a tray, heading for her business table. Eustacia converged on her, meeting her at the table.

"Hi." Carla grinned. "Sit down! Sit down! Want some?"

Eustacia shook her head.

"Got in late myself. Haven't had my dinner yet. I've had the most wonderful day with a man. Name's Emil. This time it's gonna be different. I know it!" Then with a twist of her face, "At least now I do."

"I'm glad someone had some luck today, Carla."

"What's happened now?"

"Nothing, and everything." Eustacia discovered she had picked a pickle off Carla's plate. She looked at it slightly bewildered and then began to explain what had happened.

"When the girls arrived this evening," she concluded, "that just kind of brought it all home to me, Carla. What am I going to do if I never find Philip? How will we live with that? How will I provide?" Eustacia heard the ragged tone coming into her voice, and she clamped her lips shut.

"Now, you listen. First of all, you *are* providing. You're making good wages driving the stage, so you don't have to worry about that. Leastways not now. Second, there's bunches of mines and miners sprinkled through these hills that you haven't seen yet. You only scraped the top of the pot, hon."

"True, Carla, but I don't know how to reach many of them. I can't find my way around the back hills. I'm as much a greenhorn as Philip is." Suddenly she stopped. It was the first time Eustacia had acknowledged that prospecting, Calico, and the Mojave had not been for Philip—that he was ill-prepared and had been wrong to come.

Avoiding the thought, Eustacia continued, "Now there also is the children's supervision to consider. What about the hours after school is dismissed? I can't leave them on their own in a wild silver camp. Carla, *you* know Calico! It's bad enough they'll be alone while I make the Calico-Daggett run. Ophelia and Collette are at very impressionable ages, each in her own way—Ophelia's interest growing in young men, Collette wanting to know about everything around her without regard to danger." Pickle juice was dripping off Eustacia's fingers. She grimaced and set the pickle back on the edge of Carla's plate. "I beg your pardon."

Carla swallowed a wad of mashed potatoes, then pushed at another portion with her fork. "I could watch them," she casually offered.

"You?" Eustacia fell silent. The tears that she had been holding back all day began to well behind her eyes.

"Now listen, Eustacia Kibbe, you got nothing to worry about. I know what decent is! Once a whore don't mean always a whore." The second portion of potatoes found its way into Carla's mouth.

"No! Carla, I wasn't thinking any such thing!" Eustacia felt the tears really ready to come now. "I just never expected such unselfishness, such an offer. I mean, you have this new man, and you've never had children—oh, dear, I expect that's another blunder, too. Oh, Carla, all I want to do is cry!"

"You can't," Carla snapped. "Not here. Not now, or everything will be blown for you. And it's no blunder about children. Best I never had them. Took pains after—well, you know what after, Eustacia—to make sure there were none—one way or another." Carla waved with her fork as if to brush aside all that had been said. "Now all we need to do is solve the problem of a guide for you." Carla put down her fork and dabbed her mouth with a napkin. "And I think I see him coming."

Grant Whitman walked up behind Eustacia. He took his hat off, nodding at Carla. "Excuse me, Carla, Stash. I've been thinking about what we said at Bismarck today, Stash. We're both looking for people, and eventually, going our separate ways, we're going to cover the same ground. For some of it we could ride together. And then, while you're driving the stage, I could keep my ears open for any helpful information about your brother, Philip."

Eustacia looked at Carla. Carla's nod was almost imperceptible.

Eustacia hesitated a moment, swiftly weighing the pros and cons of the arrangement. With such close contact, sooner or later Grant was bound to discover her disguise. She believed he may have already suspected from the first day. Then what? Then maybe nothing. He had made no move so far. He certainly did know the Mojave area. Then there was the picture of two damp heads resting on pillows and Collette's small voice asking about Daddy. Why was she hesitating? Earlier she had been wishing for help—Grant's help, if she were honest.

Eustacia nodded. "I agree to your proposition, Grant."

Chapter Seven

By the time Eustacia had finished her morning Daggett run and appeared back at Yung Hen's, Ophelia and Collette were dressed in their muslin school dresses, long sleeves tapered snugly at the wrists, and were sitting alone at the end of the long table in the dining room. Their porridge bowls were empty in front of them, and they were finishing their toast and debating the merits of drinking their prune juice.

Yung Hen came up behind them, cutting the lively argument short. "You drink."

Ophelia glanced up at the man, her mouth bridling slightly, but when faced with his firm impassivity, she reached out her hand and picked up her juice glass. She knew she was not going to have a nice time in Calico. Collette simply grinned and followed her sister's lead. She secretly liked prune juice.

Eustacia, standing in the hallway, smiled to herself, feeling more assured about her girls' presence in the silver camp. They had already encountered one firm hand that not even Ophelia could bluff. Eustacia knew she could count on Yung Hen's watchfulness. The

Chinese man saw everything and, she suspected, knew everything in Calico.

Eustacia strode into the dining room. "All right, girls, time for school. Finish up."

The girls drained their glasses, then pushed their chairs back, standing and pulling their shawls around them.

"Now remember," Eustacia instructed. "When school is out, you are to walk immediately to the Hurdy-Gurdy House. The front will be locked, but you go down the alley to the back door. That leads to the kitchen. Carla will let you in. She promised a snack, too. Then you get to work on your lessons. There's plenty of room at that kitchen table."

"Mother, I really don't think the Hurdy-Gurdy is an appropriate place for us to be. I overheard about its goings on this morning at breakfast."

Eustacia shot Yung Hen a look.

He shrugged as if to say, "I cannot bridle men's mouths."

"I am certainly not asking you to become a working girl, Ophelia," Eustacia replied dryly.

"Then, of course, this Miss Maxey cannot be the best sort—proper, you know, to run a place like that." The only thing that saved Ophelia's priggishness from being outlandish was that she did not sniff like some girls in English novels.

"I am not going to discuss Carla's merits or demerits with you, Ophelia—at least not now. But I insist you be polite and obedient. That is the mark of a true lady. Now, let us get along."

Ophelia was silent as she fell in behind her mother and Collette. She knew from her mother's tone of voice that she had no hope of continuing the conversation.

In front of Yung Hen's, Grant surfaced out of the congested street. He was leading two horses, his own and one that bore the Delameter brand. "Hey, Stash," he called.

Eustacia stopped and waited for him. Grant looped the reins around a post and climbed up onto the boardwalk. As soon as he was within conversational distance, Eustacia took the initiative. "These are my two nieces, Ophelia and Collette. We're on our way to enroll in school. Then I'll be ready to leave."

"I'll walk along with you, if you don't mind. We can leave from the schoolhouse."

Eustacia nodded.

Collette's eyes were wide and locked on the horses as Grant fell in step with the trio, leading the two animals as he walked in the street beside the boardwalk—which in itself was no mean trick considering the traffic. Grant caught on instantly.

"How about letting the little one have a ride to school, Stash? She'll be safe enough with me leading."

Collette's face lit like a beacon.

Eustacia smiled, remembering her own love for and fascination with horses. "Collette may ride," she replied.

They all stopped. Grant picked Collette up and settled her on his own horse, showing her how to clamp hold of the pommel. "I know my own nag, Stash, but not too much about the one I borrowed from the warehouse for you," Grant explained.

Then Collette captured his attention. She had a hundred questions: What was the horse's name? Was he a stallion or a gelding? What did he eat? How often did he eat? Did horses really sleep standing up? Grant, for his part, gave serious attention to them all, answering patiently and at length. He liked the little girl. She was eager and pretty. He liked her also because she was her mother's child.

At one point, Grant looked up at Ophelia on the

boardwalk as if he sensed a note of annoyance in her. He smiled wryly at both her and Eustacia. "If Collette doesn't ask or get an answer, she'll never learn anything."

Ophelia blushed as if she'd been caught at some wrongdoing, but she remained convinced he was trying to justify his infatuation—infatuation with her mother. It was a well-known fact that if a man wanted to win a woman with children, he should first win the children over. What had been going on between Eustacia and this man while she was supposed to be looking for her husband? Then she reluctantly gave her mother the benefit of the doubt. Perhaps it was all innocent. Perhaps her mother didn't even notice this man's interest. She certainly didn't look like she did.

Eustacia's face might have been a mask. She was far away in her thoughts, wondering what news her telegram to her father would bring and how she was going to explain the girls to Grant—in fact, she was rehearsing her explanation.

"Well, here we are," Grant said, interrupting Eustacia's thoughts. "Let me help you off, Collette." He grasped the little girl's waist and swung her down into the schoolyard.

Their arrival had been a guaranteed attention getter. Clusters of children formed around the perimeter, ranging from some of Collette's age to a very few of Ophelia's, the boys dressed in collarless shirts and pants with suspenders, the girls in muslin dresses not all that dissimilar from the Kibbe girls'. There was a little whispering, mostly among the girls, but the boys, upon realizing there were going to be no new male schoolmates, broke away to play.

"I'll just be a minute speaking to Miss Mooney, Grant." Eustacia shepherded the girls up the front steps of the schoolhouse.

A few minutes later, Eustacia was on her way back, Miss Mooney and the girls trailing after her as far as the porch. Briskly, the schoolteacher clanged the handbell, and the children swarmed toward the steps, Eustacia dodging small bodies as though they were darts. When she reached Grant and the horses, he was chuckling.

"I wouldn't want to get caught in that stampede!"

Eustacia joined in his laughter and then swung her gaze back to the schoolhouse. The children had formed two almost-orderly lines, one for boys, the other for girls, with some surreptitious shoving and whispering going on.

"Ophelia's unhappy," Eustacia remarked.

"Why?"

"She says she's too grown up for the school, that I should see that for myself since there are so few here her age. I explained that she needed to continue her education and that perhaps there just weren't that many families in Calico with children her age. The term 'children' did nothing to improve her disposition."

Grant looked concerned. "Is she giving you real trouble, Stash?"

Eustacia wrinkled her nose, her eyes squinting. She looked puzzled. "No, not yet. Come on, let's go, Grant. Where are we bound for?"

"Borate."

"I've heard the name bandied about. What's Borate?"

"I've been doing my homework, too, mostly because on the day Arango killed my dad, he and his bunch seemed to head off in the direction of Mule Canyon."

"What's Mule Canyon?" Eustacia asked.

"Mule Canyon is where this mining region got its start. It's a long story."

"It would certainly pass the time while we ride. Besides, we may discover a clue in the information we already have." Eustacia swung into the saddle of her borrowed mount. The horse shifted around in a half circle, as if judging his rider, then responded as Eustacia directed him in beside Grant's animal.

Silently Eustacia and Grant rode out of the schoolyard and a few minutes later out of Calico, heading east. Once on the trail, Grant picked up his story. "I've been talking to Harv Miller and to Luke Portage down in Daggett, and this is what I get. Back in '81, when the silver strike was made, many prospectors found their way into the canyon. They discovered veins of white crystalline rock, knew it wasn't silver, and moved on. But the carpetbaggers, so to speak, came on their heels, filed claims on the deposits, and sold them to unsuspecting greenhorns who wouldn't have the faintest idea in what kind of rock to find silver."

With a twinge of guilt, Eustacia thought Philip would have fallen into that category. She sighed, then pushed the thought away, reaffirming to herself that one person, no matter how good, couldn't be everything.

"Then in '83, a Texas miner by the name of H. B. Stevens did some silver prospecting in the area. He couldn't figure out what kind of ore he was looking at, and so he sent a sample up to an assayer in San Francisco. Talk about your original bait and switch, Stash, the next part of the story comes pretty close to it. The assayer didn't respond to Stevens. Instead he told a friend named Coleman—who has turned out to be something of a borax pioneer—that he had a pretty clean sample of borate of lime. He also told him where he got it. Coleman moved quickly. He sent a man to Calico to quietly buy up all those useless silver claims from the stuck greenhorns, who probably thought themselves pretty clever to unload them on someone dumber than themselves. Coleman got the whole canyon for under twenty thousand dollars. He began developing mines in the canyon and hauling the borax out by mule team to the main line at Daggett, twelve miles away. The huge number of mules and the nonstop cussing being done at them by the skinners are responsible for Mule Canyon getting its name. Borate is the local supply camp for the borax miners. The town's had a lot of changes in the last year."

"How come?" Eustacia asked.

"Well, for one thing, Coleman went bankrupt last year, and Borax Smith took over the properties. He's been building Borate up. The talk is he might settle in himself—at least on a sporadic basis. So maybe he just wants things nice. You'll see. Borate's not a big town, certainly nothing like Calico, but I'm told it has a boardinghouse that will handle two hundred, a post office, a store, and a blacksmith. There are cabins for married miners, but some of the others are still living in dugouts in the clay hills. Those are the ones I'd like to talk to. They're far enough out where they might have seen something. Also the mule skinners, with the traveling they do between Borate and Daggett, are another possibility."

"It sounds like you have it all figured out, Grant."

Grant's grin slipped off his face. "It sounds good. What we actually get could just be one long string of noes."

Eustacia nodded, a little deflated. That certainly had been her experience to date. She began paying closer attention to the terrain, now that they were close to Mule Canyon and Grant had stopped talking. The desert was gray-white, loose rubble salted among the drab olive sagebrush. The hills around had the same low foliage until they entered Mule Canyon. There the canyon walls were slick clay, eerily tinged with green, lavender, purple, and ocher deposits. They followed the steep, deeply rutted, narrow road that twisted over the canyon's undulating slopes. As should have been expected, they met head-on with a loaded wagon being drawn by a twenty-mule team. Actually, they heard the skinner's string of expletives long before the first mule topped the rise.

As Grant pulled his horse out of the rutted track up onto a shallow slope, he grinned at Eustacia. "Amazing, isn't it, the command he has of language!"

Eustacia chuckled. "I just wonder if it makes any difference to the mules."

The mule skinner was long on crust and short on patience. Grant hallooed him, but he kept right on moving, never missing a beat in his long string of adjectives. As he pulled abreast Grant, he interrupted himself long enough to shout, "What you want?"

"Information. Have you seen a sizable body of men moving around in these parts?"

"Nope."

"How about signs of a big camp?"

"Nope."

"How about a stranger, anyone, buying an extraordinary amount of supplies?"

"Nope."

Now Grant was shouting at the tail of the wagon. "Ever hear of anyone named Philip Kibbe—greenhorn prospector?"

"Nope." The mule skinner twisted around on his seat. "Look, bud, I make three round trips in two days looking at the rear ends of these nasty, stubborn critters. I ain't got time nor eyes for anything else, nor for being nosey. I got my hands full right here. These ain't the most agreeable companions."

"I hear camels are worse," Grant called back, but the skinner had gone back to his one-sided conversation with the mules.

Eustacia was laughing, despite the negative answers they had received to Grant's questions.

Grant grinned, too. "See what I meant, Stash, about 'no' answers?"

"Maybe it will be better in Borate." Eustacia kneed her horse back into the narrow road, still chuckling. She would like to have seen the skinner driving twenty spitting camels.

They rode through Borate, and it was much as Grant had said. There were a few women on the street, heading in and out of the store and the post office. There were also men, but not near the amount in Calico. Both Eustacia and Grant figured most were underground in the mines. Neither was the horse-drawn traffic as great, mostly consisting of long strings of mule teams pulling out for Daggett. Eustacia thought Borate was a nice town, but it was a company mining town with none of the promise of quick riches that buoyed existence in a silver camp like Calico.

Just beyond the town limits, a waste dump, a hill nearly forty feet high, signaled the proximity of the first mine. They saw some miners, stripped to the waist, gathered in a clearing that was hedged with small heaps of rock.

"Want to give it a try?" Grant asked.

Eustacia nodded. "We're going to stop at all the mines, so we might as well take them in order."

As they reined in at the clearing, one of the miners detached himself from the others. Now Eustacia understood why they were standing around. The miner held a battered tin pail in one hand and a doughy roll encasing a slab of cheese in the other. She could see a half-empty bottle of beer in the pail and a tin of some kind of fish. Eustacia glanced overhead. Yes, it was noon, and the men were having their lunch.

"Help you folks?" the miner asked.

Grant quickly went through the repertoire of questions he used on the mule skinner and got the same results. Then the miner added, "You might ask some of the others, especially Big Ben. I don't get out of Borate much, except for a night on the town in Daggett once in a bit. Got me a room at the boardinghouse. But Big Ben, he's still clinging to that dugout in the canyon wall he made for himself when he came in '81. Guess home's where you find it."

"Where do we find Big Ben?" Grant asked.

"Down in the mine. Takes his lunch in with him. Myself I can't see it. Need a little daylight and air. But some of the others stay down, too. Want to go in?"

"Yes," Eustacia replied.

"How about just I go, Stash?" Grant suggested. For some reason he didn't feel comfortable about Eustacia going into the mine. It wasn't a woman's place.

"No," she said. "This is my quest, too. A partnership was what you suggested last night."

Grimly, Grant reminded himself that Eustacia didn't know he was aware of her secret. It greatly hampered any argument he might have against her going, so he clamped his lips shut and dismounted.

Eustacia fell in behind the men. They strode over to the main entrance, a rough hole in the hillside framed into a square by timbers. Wearily the miner put down his tin pail, hanging on to his half-eaten sandwich though, and picked out a candle from a box. Grant struck a match and lit it, then lit two other candles for himself and Eustacia.

"Come on then," the miner said.

They were a good piece down the main tunnel when Eustacia saw several men grouped around a barrel.

The barrel stood against a shoring timber, pushed as far to the side as possible to allow free movement down the tunnel.

"What are they doing?" she asked.

The miner twisted his neck around to look at the boy. "Oh, they just finished handling explosives, and they're washing the nitroglycerin off so they can eat. Big Ben should only be a little bit past."

As they drew closer to the men, one called, "Hey, Orly, company ain't going to like you bringing non-employees down."

"That sounds like Ben himself," Orly commented to Grant and Eustacia. Then he called back, "What harm can come? We got a clean operation here. No gas or nothing. Besides, they want to talk to you, Ben, and you're such a mole there's no other way."

They had reached the barrel now. Some of the men trickled past them, headed above ground. Orly stopped near the barrel, cramming a corner of roll and cheese into his mouth. As Eustacia slid around him, Grant behind her, she idly noticed that the water in the barrel had been used so often that it was thick with mud. How could the miners consider their hands clean washing in *that*?

Orly was busy talking, full mouth and all, to one of the miners just wiping his wet hands on his overalls. The man laughed and slapped Orly's arm. Suddenly Orly's candle was skimming the barrel surface. There was a flash and a booming thunderclap, which echoed and echoed. It was punctuated by the ripping and splintering of wood, followed by the ferocious groan and then rush of rock.

The thick mud water splashed Eustacia, and she was hit along one side of her face by a slat of flying wood. Numbed, she looked up and saw the rock ceiling shifting. Then through the rain of dust she saw an arm reach out, and she was roughly shoved backward. She fell, and because small rocks began pelting her, she rolled and rolled, farther down the tunnel, she thought. The noise was deafening, and she clamped her hands over her ears, tucking her face toward her chest. *It has to stop sometime!* she kept thinking. *It has to stop!*

Eventually the noise faded, diminishing itself in repeated distant echoes. The dust lessened, and the ground solidified once more. Eustacia untucked her chin, cautiously lowered her hands, and sat up. It was dark; her candle had been blown out. No, she had lost it!

She took a deep breath, trying to quell the panic, and choked on dust for her efforts. Firmly, between gasps for air, she told herself that if she could take over the runaway San Bernardino stage, she could get herself out of this. All she had to do was get herself back up the tunnel to the others. There she hit a snag. Which direction was the correct way?

Eustacia cast around in the dark, groping over the rough floor and sharp pieces of rubble for her candle. She found nothing and figured she must have dropped it when she was shoved. Who had shoved her anyway, and why?

The groping, however, had solved part of her plight. She had detected a slight downward grade to one side of her. That must mean that way led farther into the mine. She hitched around and began crawling in the opposite direction, calling as she went. Her voice only bounced back at her. She refused to hear its mocking.

Eustacia never expected to find her candle, but by chance she laid her hand right on it. It was smooth and greasy, in contrast to the sharp rock and grainy dust. At the same time, she heard a deep groan in the heavy atmosphere. She fumbled in her pockets, found an old match, prayed that the sulfer on it was still good, and struck it. It burned true. She caught her breath. It hadn't occurred to her until now that there might be a limited supply of oxygen. She promptly lit her candle and waved out the match.

The small light flickered over the wrecked mine tunnel. She crawled around in a circle, illuminating the rubble, until she found the source of the groan she had just heard. Ironically, what Eustacia first saw was Orly's hand still clutching part of his sandwich. She crawled to him. His head and shoulders were clear, but he was trapped from the waist down by debris. The hand that had held his candle had been blown apart. He was breathing steadily, though he seemed barely conscious, which Eustacia thought a blessing.

Then she remembered that the man called Ben had been standing close to them. Again, she swung the candle around. She found him, and that was when the heart went out of Eustacia. She could only see a little bit of clothing sticking out from under the burial mound of rock and timber. Both the ceiling and the wall had been blown on top of the man. Whatever information he might have known, if indeed any, was lost with him.

Eustacia began to tremble. She had been standing so close to both of them. How had she escaped? Then she remembered the shove. Someone had pushed her beyond the blast, probably just as the ceiling and wall had begun to crumble. She had a pretty good idea who was responsible: Grant Whitman. But where was he now?

Eustacia was alive, but she was far from all right. She was trapped in this little dark place, sealed away from the mine entrance. She had no idea how much air she had. She knew her candle wasn't going to last long.

She couldn't go back the way she had come. Miners usually didn't dig back doors. Besides, her light would fail her even before she found a branching tunnel that might lead around the blockage. She and Orly were going to die here in the dark just as surely as Ben had.

Tears streaked down her dusty cheeks. Her throat felt so tight that she thought she was going to choke, and she began sucking fast shallow breaths, her chest heaving. She began to feel lightheaded, as though her soul were already passing from her body. *No! Not yet!* she silently screamed, and then she really was screaming, "Grant! Someone! Please! Please! Come help!" The noise careened off the walls, and Eustacia found herself pressing her palms over her ears again, as though she were the only sane person in a babbling asylum.

Her screaming eventually passed, leaving her exhausted. Wearily she dropped her hands into her lap, focusing on the small candle flame. Her children were going to be orphans. The thought stopped her cold. She had no tears—just dawning knowledge. She was facing her own death, but by calling Ophelia and Collette orphans, she had admitted to herself that Philip was already dead. If he were, then there was no hope for their children except from herself. *She had to make it!*

Eustacia crawled back to the cave-in, avoiding the mound above Ben. The acrid smell from the blast still lingered. She wondered what had happened as she moved the candlelight over the piled rubble. She was going to have to dig herself out or, if that was too ambitious, at least make a small hole to call through and so that she could breathe if the air went bad. There had to be miners on the other side—Grant, too, if he hadn't been buried. But she couldn't let herself think of that possibility. He *had* to be on the other side.

Eustacia found a little niche in the tunnel wall,

dripped wax on it, and planted the candle. Then she began pushing away the small pieces of rock until she had a pyramid behind her. That left the large boulders and sharp flat slabs. She tried pulling on one. It didn't budge. Her eyes flickered to the mound and saw a long timber, and she thought she had her solution. She tried to reach the piece of timber without stepping on the loose debris. She could not, and gingerly, hoping not to disturb anything, she worked herself up the unstable slope. Her fingers closed around the wood, splinters digging into her flesh. She pulled on the timber, and it gave a little, but did not come free. Bracing herself as much as possible, she yanked. With sudden ease and speed, it slid at her. She staggered, then tumbled off the mound, the timber knocking her elbow, then flying to the tunnel floor beside her.

For a moment, Eustacia lay still, dust specks floating down around her. When she decided she wasn't hurt, she sat up and rubbed her elbow. Then she grasped the wood, found her feet, and marched back to the pile of rocks. Climbing up on the pile, she wedged one end of the timber under a flat slab below her and levered downward. The slab moved and then, with more pressure, slid out of position and into the pyramid of small rocks. Eustacia smiled, and with a practiced eye, looked for another likely candidate. She felt better now. She had struck her first blow for freedom and had won.

Immediately following the explosion, Grant and a few of the miners had picked themselves up off the ground. From the entrance they could hear shouts of "Cave-in!" and running feet. Grant hoped that whoever was coming had enough presence of mind to bring picks and shovels. The main tunnel had a new wall—right in the middle of it.

The little group stood stunned, coughing, the dust settling around them. Grant finally asked the man standing closest to him, "What happened? What caused the explosion?"

"You know that barrel of water we were washing our hands in? Well, it was pretty thick with mud and nitro particles, probably even some were floating on the surface. Orly, poor soul, musta touched his candle to them. They're goners—Orly, Ben, and the boy with you. Goners."

Grant wished the miner would stop saying that. It was his fault Eustacia was on the other side of that wall. Yet he felt he had had no other choice. When the explosion erupted, Eustacia was barely clear of the collapsing roof. He could not yank her back to him because the debris was starting to fall between them, so he had shoved her headlong. After that he hadn't been able to see what had happened because of falling rock and billowing dust.

She should have been clear, Grant told himself. *She had to be clear.* Then Grant realized how important it was to him that Eustacia Kibbe be alive and well. For a moment, Grant almost forgot about Philip.

Miners pounded up from behind carrying picks and shovels. Hurriedly, as they eyed the obstruction, they were told the story. Impatiently, Grant urged, "Let me have a pick. Let's get started."

"Not so fast, young fella. Let's try and get a sounding first," an older miner responded. "We don't want to start in the wrong spot and cave in rock on someone."

"How are you going to do that?" Grant asked.

"I didn't say we'd be successful. Depends on how thick this rubbish is. We'll start by tapping—*carefully*—on the rock. Then we'll yell."

The older miner gently tapped the width of the slide with his pick, waiting a few seconds after each test. There was no response. Then some of the others began to yell, "Orly! Ben!" Grant added his own call: "Stash!"

The only sound was a scuttle of loose pebbles.

The old miner was again judiciously studying the slide. Thinking out loud, he said, "It looks to me like the blast came from the right wall and took out that part of the roof first. So if anyone is caught, that's the most likely place they'd be. Let's start on the other end. Rock's probably less thick there, too."

Surprisingly, the men dropped their tools and formed a brigade. Then Grant saw why. They started passing loose rocks out of the way. The man at the end was sent for candles, and Grant stepped into his place.

After the loose debris had been cleared, the miners fell back, giving the older man room. He picked his spot and let the pick fly. As rubble accumulated, the brigade formed again, clearing it away. When the old miner tired, another took his place, until all had been to the wall. On his turn, Grant was lucky. Panting, he took his last swing. The spike punctured the slide and locked into the other side. Grant was jerked forward, his midsection punching itself on the handle. He hardly felt it, though. They had the beginnings of a hole!

The old miner guffawed, "Ah, we finally softened it up enough for you, huh, young fella!"

"That you did," Grant rejoined, grinning. One of the other miners was busy unsticking Grant's pick for him, enlarging the initial break with his efforts.

Suddenly their comradery was cut short.

"Somebody! Somebody, can you hear me?" The voice was muffled and dense, but there was no mistake— it was coming through the break.

Everyone fell silent, straining their ears.

The call came again, "Hey, anybody!"

Grant pushed himself forward. "I think it's Stash."

The old miner nodded. "Sounds like a boy, not at all like Orly or Ben."

"We're coming," Grant shouted. He tried to look through the small hole, maybe all of four inches in diameter. All he could see was a little pinpoint of light in the darkness. "Stash! Stash!"

"Grant? Thank the Lord!"

"What about Orly and Ben?"

"Ben's dead. He's buried under the rock fall."

The old miner was nodding wisely, pointing to the other end of the slide.

"Orly, he got blown farther into the tunnel. He's half buried. His hand . . . well, he's badly hurt, if not dead. Can you hurry?"

"We're doing the best we can."

"Get outa the way, young fella." The old miner shouldered Grant aside. "Now, look here, boy, give your side of the slide a good going over. Can we give it a good lickin', or do we have to be careful about more cave in?"

There were a few minutes' silence. The tension built, and some of the miners shifted uneasily, crunching gravel under their boots. "Shh!" the miner at the hole growled.

Then Eustacia's voice came back. "It looks pretty stable right here. I wouldn't vouch for the other end. It's pretty hard to see. My candle's going out—right now!"

Grant heard the panic in the shrill upturn of those words. He shouted encouragingly, "It won't be long now!"

"All right, boys, let's get at it," the old man ordered. "We got us a boy 'fraid of the dark to bail out." He said it good-naturedly. There wasn't one of them who would have felt any different from the boy.

The work went quickly after that, shifts of four

miners banging away at the now weakened rock, the others carting away the pieces. The hole widened visibly, then suddenly, there was a shout. "Stop swinging! You'll hit him!"

Grant looked over the shoulders of others and saw Eustacia bellying her way out, feet first. When her head had cleared the passage, she stood up, panting, her words halting. "I'm sorry. Not another minute. I just couldn't."

The old miner clapped his hand on Eustacia's shoulder. "That's okay, kid, we all feel the same way." Then he and the rest turned back to what, all thought now, was a grim job.

Eustacia saw Grant and moved toward him. The miners made way. Grant grasped her upper arm. "Come on, let's get you some fresh air. Are you all right?" He was piloting her out of the mine. Reinforcements carrying more equipment, including tarps, closed in behind them.

"Just some scrapes and bruises. It would have been the end if you hadn't shoved me, Grant."

"I wish I could have done something for Orly and Ben."

"Let's just go home." They were outside. Eustacia looked tired and drawn under the dirt. For a quick heartbeat Grant saw her lean toward him and thought she was going to rest her head on his shoulder. Then, as if startled, she righted herself.

"You need something to glue you together first, Stash. A stimulant." Grant glanced around and recognized Orly's lunch pail. He reached inside and pulled out the half bottle of beer. It was warm; he could tell by the feel of the glass. He held it out to Eustacia.

"No, I couldn't. Not his."

"Yes, you will. You need it for the ride back."

Grant didn't bother mentioning that apparently some-one had already pocketed Orly's tin of fish.

Eustacia took the bottle and tipped it to her lips. In four gulps it was gone. She felt warm and flushed, but also full, as though she had just eaten. Carefully she set the bottle back in the pail.

"All right, now, if you want to go," Grant offered.

"No, let's wait a few minutes to find out about Orly. He didn't seem to have much chance, but then . . . they should be reaching him soon."

Grant leaned back against one of the mine portals and folded his arms. He was so relieved that at this moment he could give Eustacia anything. *Whoa, boy,* he admonished himself. *You act like you're in love with her.* Ruefully he thought about bad timing and an unaccounted-for husband.

Then he forced away the thought, thinking instead that any further delay would cause Eustacia to be late for the afternoon stage run. That she had forgotten all about it was maybe a sign, after this experience, that she should not attempt driving a stage today.

Half an hour later, someone came out of the mine. Grant stopped him, asking the one word question, "Orly?"

"They got to him, and he's still alive. Can you beat that! Breathin' regular enough. Hand will probably come off, and below the waist he's bruised up real bad, but the foreman says he's seen worse in his day and that Orly'll probably make it."

Eustacia sighed, "Now we can go home, Grant."

As Grant pushed himself away from the portal, he found himself wishing he and Eustacia could really go home.

They were silent all the way across the darkening Mojave into Calico. Just as they came up Wall Street,

Eustacia said, "I guess I'd better check in at Mojave Station and see if I still have a job. I've just missed a run."

Grant didn't say anything, just kept his horse in step with hers and stopped in the yard when she did. Curry came out of the station house and stated the obvious. "You missed your drive, Stash. Eberson took her out, complaining all the way. He had some right too, considering his eyes ain't what they were."

Caught off guard, Eustacia asked, "He told you?"

"No. I guessed when he asked for this job. Then I heard it from a guy from San Bernardino, recently arrived." Curry looked the boy up and down in the mellow light pooling from the station house. "But you look like you have a bit to complain about yourself. What happened? If it's a good enough story and the truth, you might still have a job."

Grant cut in and began to talk. Curry just listened. He was getting used to people talking for Stash—first Eberson, now Grant. In the end, Curry yawned and said, "See you for the morning run, Stash." Then he went back into the station house for his supper of stew and fried potatoes.

Eustacia started to dismount. "Might as well return the horse here. The warehouse is only up a bit."

"I'll bring it back later."

"Thanks, Grant."

As silently as they had come into town, they rode back through it until Eustacia stopped at the alley between Yung Hen's and the Hurdy-Gurdy House. "Carla is watching my nieces," Eustacia explained as she dismounted, tossing the reins at Grant.

Just then the Hurdy-Gurdy's back door burst open, and Ophelia stormed out. Collette bobbed into the doorway, then Carla plowed into view, maneuvering around the younger girl like a river around a boulder. "Come here, young lady!"

Ophelia whirled. "I don't have to listen to you, you old . . ." And then she caught her tongue. She had not seen her mother behind her in the dimness, but somehow she could not bring herself to get out the rest of the name.

Carla, who had also not seen Eustacia, squared off in front of the rebellious girl. "Your mother has left you in my safekeeping, and safe is what I mean to keep you. I know all about young blood."

Ophelia turned pink.

"And the pretentiousness of being half grown-up. You think you know a lot! You got nothing but fool romantic ideas in your head, and sooner or later they're going to get you in trouble. You don't have any judgment, either. Take it from someone who's taken the first course over and over again."

"My mother's a romantic. She's always said so."

"But she learns, separates fact from what she would like to see. Now you listen to me, missy, you're in my care and, by God, you'll do as I say—long as it's decent, to reassure your dirty little mind—until this is over with. We might as well have it out now and here, 'cause I don't want to do this every time. And I ain't above using force, Miss Ophelia."

The girl stood stock still. Then suddenly she sensed something else. She half crooked her head, saw her mother and the shadow of a man and horse. That man was Grant, no doubt. How much had they heard?

Carla followed Ophelia's gesture and wondered the same thing. She held her ground.

Eustacia moved forward, standing beside but a little in front of Ophelia. "You will apologize to Miss

111

Maxey." Eustacia was thinking that everything Carla had said was true.

Grant nudged his horse and the borrowed one back toward the warehouse. He saw a bustle full of trouble in Ophelia.

Chapter Eight

Francisco Arango sat in the saddle, his horse pointed toward Daggett, waiting for Philip to return from his latest rendezvous with Carla. He smirked every time he thought of the two of them together. But Philip's diversion had worked. Carla had not turned Arango and his men in to the authorities, and although Arango continued to move his camp over the Mojave, he still felt his safest place was Carla's ranch.

The Mojave was definitely cooling off, not just with the encroaching evening but also with the season. It would be more comfortable, Arango thought, to be south in Mexico for the winter. He needed a lot of money for that, though—more than he had accumulated and spent to date. All of what he had done so far were small endeavors. He needed plenty of dollars to grease the grasping hands of Díaz's government and to properly arm his men for a new assault on Mexican power.

Since the Reynold Whitman killing, Arango had made himself scarce, partly to cool the Americans' memories, partly because Philip had heard that the old

113

man's son was asking questions about him. One man could do nothing against him, Arango was assured, but still he chose to play for time. Now, he decided, he felt right putting into action his plan to steal the silver off the Wells Fargo railroad car.

Philip and his horse loped through the waves of shadows like graceful swimmers. He plunged into a square of sunshine, saw Arango waiting for him, dark like a bug on the pale Mojave, and raised his arm at the distant figure. For his part, Arango looked at Philip and saw why women liked him. Despite his weakness, Philip always looked like a golden god.

The last of the sun was gone when Philip finally reached Arango—the evening a pale gray and the sunset reflecting off the mountains as though they were a prism.

"Emil!" Arango said, using Philip's assumed name. "*Buenas noches.*"

Arango noticed that Philip was certainly in an elated mood. The afternoon must have been most satisfactory. He offered the American a cigarette, knowing he would not take one.

"Now is the time to begin our great plan, Emil."

Philip looked momentarily startled.

Arango could not gauge the reaction. He did not know if Philip had been so diverted by Carla that he had forgotten their earlier talk about the railroad heist, or whether it was the suddenness of his pronouncement after so much silence. Perhaps even Philip was a little afraid about his part in the venture.

Philip recovered himself. "Finally the moment!"

"*Sí.* Tomorrow you will begin your reconnaissance of Daggett. You will need some kind of story to explain your casual questions."

"An out of work miner should do the trick."

Arango nodded and turned his horse back toward

his encampment. He was hungry. He wished for strips of white fish and red pepper laid across rice, but the pork stew would suffice.

Philip watched him go. That Arango had ridden out to meet him meant he wanted Philip on his way to Daggett now. He swung his mount around and began his mission.

Grant stood beside his wagon and thought of the smiling warehouse superintendent this morning when he had announced that Delameter Drayage had been given the contract to haul raw ore from the Sue Mine to the stamp mill in Daggett. Grant's wagon and two others were nearly done loading. The mules seemed to sense that, too; maybe it was their sensitivity to weight that told them. Their ears perpetually twitched.

"That does her," the mine foreman called.

Grant waved his hand and climbed up onto the box. The first wagon was clearing Wall Street Canyon when Grant started his mules. They responded placidly enough, and Grant thought it was going to be a pleasant ride. The day was cool and clear, the high desert air crisp and spiced with sage. He wore a second, heavier shirt over his duck-cloth one and figured that by mid-morning he'd be taking it off.

Things had also cooled down for him personally. He and Eustacia were back to normal, Stash safe in her boy disguise, and Grant realizing that until he could break through that disguise, he was stymied. Eustacia had driven away the stage, the girls had settled into their routine at Yung Hen's, although admittedly Ophelia seemed a little quiet, and the comings and goings in Calico were reassuringly normal.

It seemed to Grant that the drive was over before it had really begun. When he pulled up to the designated stamp mill, the first wagon was already half unloaded, and some of the mill laborers were starting on the second. Grant followed the foreman's hand directions and pulled his wagon into the slot alotted for him. As he wrapped the reins around the brake lever, he called, "How long?"

"Forty minutes. We got everyone working today. Southern Pacific and Wells Fargo want to pull a full express car out of here two days from now."

Grant thought he'd go over to the Daggett stage station and bum a cup of coffee off Luke Portage along with the latest news. He grinned when he realized he would be hearing all about yesterday's explosion in Borate. Then he noticed the blond-haired man standing not too far away. The man appeared to be doing nothing in particular, except watching everything. He seemed to sense Grant's appraisal, and he strolled toward him.

When he was near enough to Grant to be heard in a conversational tone, he said, "With all the activity around here, you'd think a fella could find a job. Is there any chance of getting on with your outfit? My name's Emil." He extended his hand.

Grant shook hands, also introducing himself, then added, "Afraid not. Are you out of work or just looking to change jobs?"

"Out of work miner, but I'm willing to try anything else. I've been canvassing this whole town and haven't had an offer yet."

Emil had a friendly, open smile, and Grant had forty minutes to kill. "I was just going for coffee. Want to come along?"

"I'd appreciate it. Maybe you can get me steered around straight."

"Have you tried the railroad?"

"No, not yet."

"Good. Let's go over to the Southern Pacific depot.

They've got a coffee counter there, and you can kill two birds with one stone."

A few minutes later they were sipping hot coffee from heavy, earthen mugs. The stationmaster's office door was open, and Grant heard him making arrangements with his clerk for the train and express car that were going to haul silver ingots two days hence. Car numbers for the train's makeup along with its timetable were among the overheard details; then the clerk emerged from the office and passed into the yard. By then Emil had finished his coffee and was on his feet. He gestured at the clerk's disappearing back. "Now is as good a time as any to test the water."

"Good luck." Grant waved him off with his coffee mug.

When Grant had finished his own coffee, he sauntered over to the doorway and glanced into the yard, expecting to see Emil talking to the clerk. The clerk was talking to two railroad workers, though, and Emil was nowhere to be seen. Puzzled, Grant left the depot, and as he stepped into the street, he saw Emil riding out of Daggett. He stood stock still for a moment, then turned back. It was time to talk to the stationmaster and Wells Fargo. Emil had been riding Reynold Whitman's horse.

Two days later Grant was in the express boxcar with ten hired Wells Fargo guards. Another dozen were in the passenger car directly behind, with several more up front guarding the engineer and stoker. To make the ride and, in fact, to get the powers that be to listen to him about Emil, Grant had had to disclose his true identity. There had been some quick checking with Washington via telegraph, but his clearance had come through. Now he sat against the wall with his Winchester across his knees as the train groaned and jerked forward and then picked up momentum. The others were similarly armed, except for four, who sat in the center in two teams behind a pair of rapid-fire Gatling guns, which were trained on the large sliding doors on either side of the boxcar. Arango, if he attacked, was in for some serious problems.

Grant relaxed for now and listened to the clatter of the wheels on the track. He figured Arango would wait until they were several miles into the desert so that there would be no possibility of help coming from Daggett. He wondered how Arango planned to waylay the train. Would he block the tracks or simply pull them up? The engineer had been put on guard to look for such tactics, since a derailment would only aid the Mexican bandit's plan. Grant didn't think Arango had put any men on board. He and a few of the Wells Fargo agents had looked over the boarding passengers pretty thoroughly. Grant had especially searched for Emil, because he was so obviously American and could easily infiltrate the train.

Suddenly the brakes began to squeal, and Grant scrambled to his feet as the train slowed down. He jerked open the end door, stepped onto the platform, and leaned out sideways, surveying up ahead. In a minute he was back, slamming the door and turning the key in the lock. "Tore up the track," Grant commented tersely.

Two of the Wells Fargo men were knocking out the little panes of glass in the car's two small windows. "Here they come," someone yelled. "Two directions."

Grant heard the ammunition belts clamped into the Gatlings and the metallic clatter of a half dozen Winchesters cocking. He shouldered his way to a view out one of the windows. Arango was using his favorite two-prong attack, two fans of horsemen spread out over the tracks as they flowed at the train from the rear and the front.

As the train slowed down and stopped, Grant moved back from the window and behind one of the Gatling guns. Over the hissing of the locomotive he could hear the Spanish catcalls and drumming hooves. From behind the boxcar he heard the smashing of glass as the guards at the forward end of the passenger car prepared for the attack. Standing at one of the windows in the boxcar, the head Wells Fargo agent said matter-of-factly, "Get ready."

A couple of men joined Grant's position, and two others grouped behind the other Gatling gun. Those still at the window looked questioningly at their chief. "All right," came the word, "give them one pass, and when they come closer the second time, we'll straighten out this little shindig."

Bullets began to whine, thudding into the thick wooden sides of the boxcar. Grant could hear Winchesters barking steadily from the passenger car, the men firing in relays. A stray bullet pierced the side of the express car and furrowed across the neck of one of the agents before embedding in the far wall. Blood gushed, the man reeling and falling. A man near him folded a bandanna over the gash and tied it in place with another. "Betcha that was the fault of that damn knothole I seen boardin'," the injured agent quipped. "Only one in the whole car, and a Mexican bullet finds it and me!"

"All right, they're starting on their second pass," the head agent called out. "I'll give the word when they get close."

Grant could hear firing from the front of the train. No doubt the guards in the locomotive were getting their licks in, too.

Two men stood ready near each side door, their ears straining for the sounds that would preface the order. The drumming came once again, felt more than heard, softly at first, then thundering like an earthquake.

"Now!" The order was explosive—clear and harsh.

With a snap and a metallic rattle, the doors rolled open, exposing a screen of attacking riders on either side. The Gatling guns chattered away relentlessly, the Winchesters behind them picking off anyone who was left. When the Gatling guns finished firing, there was no sound except ammunition belts being clipped into place and the snap of bullets being loaded into Winchester chambers. On either side of the train, there were nothing but bodies, rust-colored lumps on the pale Mojave. An occasional horse flitted out of range. There were no other sounds except the escaping steam of the locomotive.

Grant jumped down from the car. Some of the others followed, a few breaking off for the front of the train. Grant walked among the dead as he circled the train. He did not count how many had been killed as he looked for Arango and Emil, who were not among the bodies. He caught a loose horse and swung into the saddle, balancing his rifle in his lap like many an early frontiersman. Then he found the head Wells Fargo agent and announced, "I'll send a burial detail out from Daggett."

The man nodded. "We'll be on our way as soon as some of the boys repair that track."

The last sound Grant heard was the tamping of a spike and the gush of gravel as he turned his horse and headed for home.

Francisco Arango, Philip Kibbe, and what was left of the Mexican bandits disappeared into the rawness of the Mojave Desert. Arango stopped for no one, and as a result, he left a back trail of bodies. Over the rushing wind, Philip mentioned this to him. Arango snarled, "Do you think I am fool enough to lead them to our camp? We will ride in every direction but the right one until the dying have all dropped away, like so many fleas from the dog!"

Philip clamped his lips shut. He would only swallow wind with more words. In addition, from Arango's response, Philip felt the Mexican was angry with him. He was not wrong, as he woefully discovered after hours of riding to the dark, cold camp.

Arango's voice came out of the deep night with a hiss. "You are a fool, Philip!" He did not bother with the pretension of using the name Emil. "You have cost me many useful guns with your blundering! I send you for information, and you bring me a trap!"

"I did not know it for a trap, Francisco. The silver ingots were on the train. I heard the trainmaster himself confirming the details with his clerk!" Philip's voice did not actually squeak, but it came close.

"You did something to betray yourself! I'm sure every express car does not come furnished with two Gatling guns!" Arango's words were heavy with sarcasm.

Philip wanted to interject that perhaps Arango's continued presence in the Mojave had been the catalyst for such precautions, but he held his tongue. It was better he retained it than have Arango take it.

"I should have known better than to try to raise a storekeeper to the level of a spy!" Arango spat out. He fumbled in his pockets and found a cigarette he had rolled earlier. His fingers quivered with his anger as he tried to pinch out a few of the indentations. Defeated by the chore, he shoved the cigarette in his mouth and struck a match. In the quick light, he saw Philip's face. He looked like a white worm in Arango's eyes—a maggot.

The match light also illuminated Arango's face, and Philip almost stepped back from the naked revulsion he saw there.

"Go away from me, Philip! You bring me no pleasure." Arango turned his back on the American. He smoked steadily until he heard Philip scuff away. Then he ground out his cigarette, clenching and unclenching his fists. He must find his horse. There was a bottle of tequila in his saddlebag, and he needed it tonight.

Philip, for his part, was hurt and confused. Arango had accused him of being ineffectual, when he had brought him true information. He had called him a lowly storekeeper, as though Philip had no part in the grandeur and nobility of this revolutionary cause. Then he reminded himself that Arango was angry. He had lost many good men this day, though Philip blocked out the fact that Arango had not cared that his men had died. Perhaps Arango would forgive him tomorrow when he was rested.

Philip shuddered, as much from the Mojave cold as from his feeling of alienation. He felt like a little boy who had been stood in a corner by his father. Arango was slow to forgive. Philip had seen that many times. Perhaps if Philip could do something heroic, something to serve the cause, then Arango's forgiveness would flow. But what? So far he had only been good at procuring store goods.

This night Philip felt he needed to set his story before someone—someone who would be sympathetic, see the truth of his words, and smooth over the difficulty, as Eustacia always did. But there was no Eustacia here on the Mojave. As tired as he was, Philip saddled his horse. There was Carla. She would understand. Smiling again, Philip rode for Calico.

Philip's night was to prove luckier than his day. Eustacia, who still nightly haunted the Hurdy-Gurdy House asking questions, was stuck in Daggett. Her stage had a cracked wheel rim, and Luke Portage couldn't get repairs completed until the following morning. As for Ophelia and Collette, they had had their supper at the boardinghouse, and under Yung Hen's overseeing eye, they were now tucked safely in bed. So Philip would escape his family's detection this time, and also quickly find a possible avenue to assuaging Arango's anger.

Philip let himself into Carla's kitchen. It was late. Without even opening the door into the Hurdy-Gurdy proper, he could tell by the sounds that closing time was near. He could also tell by the utensils scattered around the cozy room that Carla had prepared a late snack. Good. He was hungry.

Philip moved to the door and cracked it open. He saw the bartender's back shifting as he put away bottles. The man must have heard the door crack, because he swung his head enough to give Philip a fishy eye. He grunted and signaled to Carla, then went back to work. He had learned a long time ago not to care about the goings on in the places he worked. He made his own life outside and took care to keep it that way.

Carla forced Philip deeper into the kitchen, widening the door opening, but blocking visibility into the room behind her bulk. "Emil! This is too risky! After today, everybody is up in arms. There's a combination of posses out looking. Was Francisco killed?" She almost hoped that.

"No, but he is very angry. He blames me. I don't see how, Carla. I got the information he wanted and betrayed myself to no one."

"Yes, you did, Emil. To Grant Whitman."

The name was oddly familiar, though Philip's tired brain couldn't make the connection.

"He saw you riding his father's horse out of Daggett. He went right to the trainmaster and Wells Fargo."

The knowledge came. Grant Whitman was the man he had had coffee with at the Southern Pacific depot. Whitman was also the last name of the rancher Arango had killed: Philip had been so stupid not to realize it all that day in Daggett. No, he had been so full of his own purpose that he just hadn't heard. "Oh, God, Carla! Pray Francisco never finds out."

"It isn't likely." Carla was thinking Emil was just like a tired little boy. He was afraid, also, and she couldn't fault him. After that day of bloodletting at her ranch, she was afraid of Arango, too.

"What's that man doing?" Philip asked, interrupting Carla's thoughts.

She knew without even catching his gesture that he was referring to Tucker, the assistant superintendent of the Run Over Mine and Mill, who was slipping in to make sure his workers were putting in no overtime at the Hurdy-Gurdy. "Checking up on his boys to make sure they're not out too late. Won't be so easy to do tomorrow, though. He'll be riding down to Daggett tomorrow afternoon to pick up the payroll. Does it every month by himself. Then tomorrow night, when the boys have been paid and have their pockets full, they won't be so easy to corral come closing time at the Hurdy-Gurdy. They settle down, though, after a couple of days when they aren't so flush."

Philip said nothing for a moment. He had his appeasing gift for Arango. He would present him with the Run Over Mine and Mill payroll.

"I'm hungry, Carla," he said. "Is there anything to eat?"

"You know there is! Just be a few minutes now."

The bartender was already taking off his apron, and Carla waved at him to lock up and go home. As the bartender headed out, Philip came up behind Carla and slipped his arms around her waist.

"I need to tell you all about everything, Carla," he whispered.

She turned and wrapped her arms around his neck.

"We'll eat, and you can begin, Emil. You can stay all night, my dear. No one will be looking for you here."

Philip turned the collar of his coat up and once more examined his revolver. He didn't want to use it, but he also suspected that Tucker wouldn't hand over the payroll just for the asking.

It was late afternoon, and gathering rain clouds were making for an early dusk. Philip was on foot in the side gully at a point where the Calico road dipped into a dry gulch, just a few feet in front of him. He was safely hidden but could easily watch the road. He heard the rattle of hooves, then in a lingering splash of sunlight saw the shadow of rider and horse, particularly Tucker's distinctive straw hat. Boldly, Philip stepped out of the shadows, revolver held high in front of him, level with the assistant superintendent's nose. "It's a pretty big looking gun, don't you think so, Mr. Tucker?" Philip politely asked.

Tucker looked to either side of him. Suddenly he realized he was in a lonely dry gulch, full darkness not many minutes ahead, and no rider behind him to come to his aid. The bandit's gun did indeed look very large and probably would make a substantial hole in a person. Tucker's thin, small lips compressed, and his face became nearly as gray as the suit he wore.

Philip sighed. "I suppose I am going to have to ask for it. Would you kindly pass down the payroll?" Philip was very pleased with his civilized and gentlemanly manner. He felt it raised the level of his highway robbery.

Tucker was thinking about the four thousand dollars and what his boss Patterson would have to say about its loss. But that did not diminish the size of the revolver he was being allowed to examine. In fact, the weapon had begun to look even larger yet. Tucker felt perspiration break out below his nose, and the payroll inside his pocket suddenly felt as heavy as a railroad car of mine debris.

"I have to reach inside my coat," he numbly responded.

"Do it, then."

Tucker did and held out a thick cloth sack tied securely at the top.

Philip accepted it, then gave himself some room, although still standing in front of horse and rider. "Now, Mr. Tucker, would you be good enough to step down? I intend to use your horse."

Tucker thought of the coming walk into Calico, stumbling his way in the dark. By the time he arrived it would be too late to organize a posse. Nevertheless, he dismounted. "Can I go?"

Philip casually waved the revolver at the assistant superintendent, shooing him on his way.

It took all of Tucker's self-control not to break into a run, but his walk was brisk enough.

For his part, Philip lost no time. He swung into the saddle and cut eastward, tucking the payroll money into a saddlebag. It was his intention to ride around the east end of the Calicos to the northern side of the mountains. Then after abandoning Tucker's horse, he planned to cross over the mountain to the heights above Calico and hide there in an abandoned mine until the Calico posse had exhausted itself. He would take no chance on accidentally leading the posse into Arango's camp. When the heat was off, he would slip down into town and collect his own mount, which Carla was caring for in a small lean-to behind the Hurdy-Gurdy.

Before Philip had gone more than five miles, the storm clouds had lowered and it was night. He stopped momentarily, wishing he had had the light a little longer, but realized the condition guaranteed no instant pursuit. He kneed his horse and continued on his way.

Rain began to fall, slowly at first, a light drizzle that insidiously soaked through his coat. When it came down harder, it obscured his vision and some of the landmarks he had noted earlier. Suddenly he was not entirely certain he was still moving eastward. Neither could he calculate how many miles he had come, though he was sure it was no safe distance. The horse was becoming restive under him. Obviously, the animal was more used to dry nights in a stall with a feed bag around his neck. The animal kept trying to turn, and Philip guessed that must be the direction of Calico.

Philip pushed on. The horse lurched as though a hoof had skidded in soft clay, then recovered. Philip slipped in the saddle and was struggling for his balance when the horse stumbled again, seeming to tangle in his own legs, and with a panicky trumpet crashed down. Philip was catapulted out of the saddle and dashed against solid rock, where he cringed away from flaying hooves as the horse tried to rise. Then the animal was up and disappearing into the dark night, carrying off the payroll, the rain quickly drowning out its hoofbeats.

Philip tried to breathe deeply, as though to exhale his shock and disappointment. The pain that seared through his chest nearly doubled him over, but that position only intensified it, so he tried to sit as still and straight as possible. He had to think, but his head hurt, and there was a buzzing in his ears. He might have a slight concussion. He certainly had several broken ribs. Also, he was rapidly being soaked to the skin, which only made his injured condition more life threatening. It was not likely the horse would return, so if Philip was going to survive, he was going to have to help himself. That meant finding shelter first, which translated into getting up on his feet.

He was shivering uncontrollably by the time he managed it. His stomach churned from the pain. Trying to decide in which direction to go, he cocked his head, hoping to hear telltale hoofbeats through the rain. All he could hear was the rush of water. He had never felt so blind and isolated in his life. Hesitantly, he took a step, then another, hoping his memory was right and he was following the horse. He would try to reach Calico and Carla. She would care for him and hide him. All the while, though, he would be on the lookout for any kind of shelter.

As the rain grew heavier, Carla slipped out of the Hurdy-Gurdy into the alley. Dazed, she leaned against the building a moment, pulling her shawl up over her head. Then she pushed herself away from the damp boards, her head bowed, and shuffled to the lean-to sheltering Emil's horse. Inside the animal shambled about its small quarters, and once it whickered.

Carla hugged herself, shuddering a little, and then leaned her forehead against the rough boards. Her eyes were closed, but that did not shut out the truth. Emil had robbed Tucker of the Run Over Mine and Mill payroll. She had hoped he would be different. Now the disappointment and the guilt Carla felt for having once again talked too much was bitter, burning like mineral salts on her tongue.

If not for the role she had played in the affair, Carla would have laughed as the rain-soaked mine official dragged himself into the Hurdy-Gurdy. He had looked a sight—all of his natty grooming and cocksureness literally washed away. There had been stunned silence as Tucker had entered the place, then one of the men from the Run Over Mine had found his legs and had rushed out to spread the word. Minutes later the mine superintendent, Patterson, had arrived, and Tucker had quickly told his story for all to hear. There had been angry shouting from the unpaid miners, and some had even smashed their empty glasses—a bill Carla was not going to forget to send to the company.

Patterson had acted quickly, forming a posse for the following morning, himself in the lead, along with some miners and a Piute tracker. Grant had also volunteered. The action had had the desired effect, settling down the enraged crowd. However, Carla thought with a smirk, diminutive Tucker buying the miners drinks had had as much influence.

With another shudder, Carla lifted her forehead off the boards. She was cold and wet by now. She did not know what she had expected the lean-to and the nearness of Emil's horse to give her. Neither would a drink be enough to deaden her pain. Tonight was a night for laudanum—for disillusionment. Soon her whole picture of Emil would be spidered with cracks, until it broke apart altogether.

The following morning, little Collette wandered out in front of the boardinghouse to watch the posse—more specifically Grant—mount up. The rain had spent itself in the night. Now sunshine was evaporating the standing puddles and raising steam from the soaked hitching rails.

The six-year-old girl liked the Mojave smells of wet sand and spicy plants, and she was smiling broadly when Dorsey, the mail dog, ran up to her, barking joyously. He plopped into a sit, tail sweeping the boardwalk, and raised one paw, his eyes pleading. Collette laughed and dug into her apron pocket for the piece of gingerbread she had saved at dinner the night before. She broke it in half, gave one piece to the eager dog, and began to nibble on the other herself. She and Dorsey had become fast friends, and because Carla firmly believed young children needed exercise, Collette was allowed to go with the dog for a short run each day.

Carla reasoned that with the dog along, no harm could come to the child. Fifteen-year-old Ophelia, too busy trying to be grown up and mooning over her lost father, never accompanied the two.

This Saturday, Ophelia was in an especially foul mood as she, too, traipsed out of the boardinghouse. Her mother had just charged her with her sister's care, which was always a bother. Moreover, it was approaching Saturday evening, and she had discovered not the slightest acceptable entertainment available to her, unlike Saturday nights in San Bernardino. She barely glanced at the dog, but Dorsey edged away from her anyway as she approached. When Grant threw a grin at Collette, which by proximity included Ophelia, the older child openly sneered, then turned away to look uptown.

Collette smiled back; then with a sidelong look at her sister, she slipped off the boardwalk, Dorsey padding behind her. She did not like being with Ophelia when she was feeling spiteful. It made so many wonderful things look out of shape—even spoiled the taste of her gingerbread. Wistfully, she watched Grant and the other men of the posse, hoping she might be invited along on their adventure, and began to drift behind them. After all, Grant had let her ride his horse once, and he was always slipping her special treats. Sometimes it was a warm and juicy meat pie or a jaw breaker or a bit of ribbon.

When the posse rode out of town, Collette was straggling far behind, distracted now and then by a sprig of sweet smelling herbs or an insect. Dorsey pranced along beside her. When Collette discovered she had lost the riders altogether, she decided to turn back with her treasures, choosing a different path so that she might find different treasures.

Back in town, when Ophelia realized there was nobody left to snub, she looked around for her sister.

Quickly she discovered that Collette and the dog were not on the boardwalk. Annoyed, she scanned the street but could see neither Collette nor Dorsey nor the posse. "Bother!" Ophelia muttered. "Now I've got to look for that imp!"

Ophelia started off into the hills after the posse. She expected to come upon Collette fairly quickly, but the miles began to slip away. She called, but there was never an answer—not from the men, Collette, or even the dog. She began to feel isolated and a little afraid in the hills. Ophelia was just about to turn back when she saw a mine opening. It appeared deserted. There was no spattering of tools around it, and parts of the raw rock were covered with growth. Would Collette have gone in there to explore? The thought made Ophelia's flesh prickle into goosebumps. For a moment more she stood undecided, then she approached the entrance. She would just glance inside and call before returning to Calico.

The sun warmed the mouth of the mine, but the air smelled of dust and chemicals and rusting metal. Ophelia, wrinkling her nose, stepped just inside, blinking rapidly as she called, "Collette! Collette! Are you in here, you little minx?"

"My Lord!" came a reply. The words, puffed with astonishment, exploded through the stale air.

Ophelia's blinking had stopped as her eyes adjusted to the dimness. Now her breath caught in her throat and squeezed back into a tight ball. She would know that beloved voice anywhere, despite its wheeziness. Hungrily, her eyes sought the shadows, until she finally saw him propped up against a timber, pale and muddy. "Daddy!"

Philip was stunned, questions welling up despite his pain. Ophelia scrambled toward him, and as she threw her arms around him, Philip cautioned, "Easy, my pigeon, I've been wrecked."

Gently, Ophelia pulled away from her father, rocking back on her knees. She could feel a tear rolling down her cheek. Yet she also wanted to laugh, to release the horrible ache in her throat and chest.

Philip's hand reached out and wiped away his daughter's tears, then caressed her blond curls, drawing her head close to him. He kissed her lightly on the forehead. Then from exhaustion his hand dropped onto her shoulder. Philip's voice was close to a whisper. "Not so long from now, you can give me that big hug we've both been needing, Ophelia, princess."

Ophelia's eyes narrowed a little in pain as they flicked over the gash on her father's forehead. "What happened to you?"

Philip grinned wanly. "A horse threw me. My head took a good conk, and there're a few broken ribs. Ophelia, I'm going to need your help. Food, water, bandages, medicine. My dearest, can you do it?"

"And keep it a secret?" Her smile was impish, and her voice already had a conspiratorial quality.

"How did you know?"

Ophelia became serious. "Because, Daddy, that is the only reason you would have stayed away so long with no word to us. If you couldn't tell us!"

Philip patted her arm. "I take it, since you're here, your mother and Collette are, too?"

"Yes, in Calico. Mother came to look for you, then Grandpa got sick and we had to follow her. Mother has the queerest job. She's driving the Calico stage—dressed as a man!"

Philip said nothing, assimilating the facts, judging how his position had been affected, trying to decide what explanation he would give his daughter—because she would surely ask for one.

"Daddy." Ophelia's voice was small and tight. "What has kept you away?"

Philip took Ophelia's hand and held it firmly. "Now, my dear, you're going to have to listen to it all and try to understand. You've always had good judgment, taking after my own ways more than your mother's—though for her part, she is a good, supportive wife, fit for the most noble."

"I'll judge," Ophelia said with her chin upraised, but her eyes said she already believed whatever her father was about to say.

"I've been aiding Francisco Arango, a great revolutionary leader of the Mexican people. I am his second lieutenant in his gallant struggle to free Mexico."

"But Arango's a bandit!" Ophelia was shocked, her mind trying to piece the information into its proper, acceptable place in the puzzle.

"Shh, my pet. Remember I said you had to listen to it all. Arango is not really a bandit. Sometimes his methods are harsh, but it is for the good of the Mexican people. It is only those who are uneducated, who have lived like you see around you, who do not understand and call him a bandit."

Silently, Ophelia thought of Grant Whitman, who called him that. And then she knew her father was correct in what he said. Besides, her father knew the Mexican personally, working closely with him. There was no contest as to who was to be believed.

Philip's rhetoric about the conditions of the people under Díaz's regime, about how an army had to have supplies whether stolen or bought with stolen money, grew more textured until it amounted to oratory. Ophelia was enthralled.

The mine was brighter and warmer by then. Ophelia could clearly see the bruised welting on her father's forehead. "How did the horse come to throw you?"

Philip told her, explaining how after hours of crawling he had finally discovered this abandoned mine.

133

"Then we must be very secret, Papa, because there is a posse out looking for you. A man named Grant Whitman and several others."

Philip wondered at the distaste in Ophelia's voice, then believed it was because his safety was threatened. "You are right, Ophelia. Let's not even tell your mother and Collette for a while. I need time to rest and think." His head fell tiredly into his hand.

With resolve, Ophelia stood up. "I will go now, but I'll be back after noon dinner with everything you need."

When Ophelia returned to Calico, she found Collette with Carla, both distraught over her disappearance. Glibly, Ophelia explained she had been searching in the hills for Collette, and then she hurried her sister off to Yung Hen's for dinner.

Yung Hen had apparently made a special purchase from the German lady who made garlic sausages, because the boardinghouse platters were heavy with them. There were also whole new potatoes, steamed cabbage with Oriental spices, plenty of coffee, milk for the girls, and brownies for desert. Ophelia served herself and couldn't believe her luck. The sausage and potatoes were easily transportable. She cleaned her plate and took a second portion.

"I've never seen you with so much appetite, Ophelia," Collette remarked.

"Must have been that hike in the hills looking for you!" Ophelia retorted tartly. She noticed Collette had eaten only about a third of her dinner. Fine. That could go, too.

Rubbing her forehead a little, Collette drank half her milk, then slipped out of her chair. "I'm going upstairs to read. Mama got a new picture book for me down in Daggett. Borrowed it from someone." Slowly, Collette drifted out of the dining room, one hand dragging up the banister.

Ophelia waited until the other boarders had also left. Then, before Yung Hen's Chinese workers came to clear the dishes, she went into action. Using her and Collette's big, blue checkered napkins, she wrapped up what was on her plate and her sister's, plus the remaining sausages and potatoes on the platter. She slipped a brownie into her pocket, dumped Collette's glass of milk into the half-full pitcher, and then skedaddled out of the dining room with it and her bundle.

Ophelia hid in the parlor across the way until the Chinese had passed with their empty metal trays, heading for the dining room. Then she scurried down the hallway and into the kitchen. It was empty, so she quickly stole some coffee, bread, bacon, a few eggs conveniently out in a bowl, and a small frying pan. These treasures she put in a Chinese marketing basket; then she poured the pitcher of milk into a jar. Finally, she rushed out the back door into the alley between Yung Hen's and the Hurdy-Gurdy House. She made for the lean-to behind the Hurdy-Gurdy and cached her load.

Next Ophelia intended to raid Carla's for the rest of her supplies, but how to get in and out undetected? Then she held her breath. The Hurdy-Gurdy's back door opened, and out Carla swooped across the alley and into Yung Hen's. Ophelia fairly dived into the Hurdy-Gurdy, scuttling across the kitchen and into the dance hall. She grabbed a bottle of brandy from under the bar, ran upstairs and snatched a couple of blankets off cots, then she pushed into Carla's room. She knew Carla had medical supplies stored somewhere, just for emergencies. Weighing speed over caution, Ophelia recklessly slammed drawers open and shut until she had purloined a roll of bandages, some salve, and a part bottle of laudanum. Back down the stairs she raced, pausing before entering the kitchen and then again before she slipped into the alley. All was clear, and Ophelia raced back to the lean-to.

She added the medical supplies to her basket, secured the jar of milk in it, and then folded the blankets and set them on top. She thought about riding the horse Carla was keeping for someone in the lean-to, then thought better of it. Better to leave horse stealing until later, when her father had recovered and needed it. Ophelia started out then, mixing nonchalantly with the uninterested Saturday crowds.

So began Ophelia's pilfering. Nightly she would creep into Yung Hen's kitchen and take what she could. Each day she hid something from breakfast and whatever she could scavenge from her and her sister's lunches, as well as from the other schoolchildren's. She had also stolen two canteens and hidden them near the schoolhouse. She carried one full of water to her father and returned with the empty one. Immediately after school she would give Collette the slip and rush into the hills. When she returned to Carla in the dusk, she had some glib story about why she had been delayed, delighted at the distrust on the woman's face, as much as by her adventure.

For Philip's part, he was enjoying the excitement as well. He marveled at Ophelia's ability and genuinely appreciated her adoration and company—perhaps all the more because their time together was stolen. She brought him news, one time telling him that the posse had found Tucker's horse. When they had discovered the payroll in the saddlebag, they had seemed less eager for the chase, Patterson averring that the scoundrel was probably dead in some ravine anyway.

Philip also saw the joke on Carla, his own daughter outwitting Carla to nurture the woman's lover, Emil. Philip's feelings for Carla were undergoing transformation. Now that Ophelia had found him, he was practically back in the bosom of his family. When he was better and more able, he would find Eustacia and explain it all. She would understand and believe him, accepting the small sacrifice she had had to make. Why, what she had undergone was no more than what women do in a war, Philip reasoned. With his family in the vanguard, he could not keep on seeing a back-street mistress. Ending his relationship with Carla should not jeopardize Arango either, because Philip guessed he would soon leave the Mojave for Mexico. So when Ophelia told Philip about Carla's posturings, he joined in her laughter.

Three days of Ophelia's slipping around was all Carla could take. She had said nothing to Eustacia, but now she was afraid not to speak. Carla suspected Ophelia was sneaking off to a young man, and a daughter in the family way would only mean more trouble for Eustacia.

The situation came to a head late one afternoon. Dusk was being pushed into the silver camp on a head of misty clouds. Eustacia, back a little earlier than usual, walked up Wall Street, Grant beside her. He usually came back now with "the boy" from Mojave Station. Carla was waiting in the boardinghouse's shadowy hallway, having just turned Collette into her bed upstairs. The little one seemed sick.

As Eustacia and Grant came through the boardinghouse doorway, Carla stopped them. "Stash, I got to talk to you about Ophelia. She's not back yet. She's been slipping off several days now. Always has some bona fide sounding excuse, but I think she's up to no good."

Eustacia wished she could have been surprised. Tiredly, she almost pulled her hat off, then remembered Grant. For days now the tension had been building between herself and her eldest daughter, and Eustacia couldn't put her finger on the why of it. Ophelia had acquired a superior manner and a sly look, and she was slow to obey and sharp-tongued. Sighing, Eustacia said, "I'll take care of it, Carla. This very evening."

Ophelia had just swung in the boardinghouse door. She looked at the three adults and instinctively knew she was in trouble. For a moment, she focused on Grant. Beligerently, Ophelia asked herself how her mother could be so disloyal to her father while *she* heroically undertook his care? Then the three realized Ophelia's presence, Eustacia pivoting slightly to face her. Ophelia lashed out first, having heard her mother's last remark. "Take care of what?" she demanded.

"You," Eustacia answered succinctly. "You will go upstairs, and we will discuss your behavior of the last week. But I tell you now, Ophelia, there will be only one result of that discussion. There will be no more slipping off—whether it's into the hills or somewhere here in Calico you've been going."

Defiantly, Ophelia eyed her mother, then biting her lower lip, she flounced past her and headed upstairs. Her mother might be able to prevent repeated trips to her father, *but there would be one last one!* After that, it wouldn't matter if she was caught and imprisoned in her room until she was an old woman!

Chapter Nine

Carla had been right about Collette being sick, but as Eustacia sat beside her, sponging her flushed cheeks and neck, she was beginning to fear it was much worse than any of them had thought. It was after dinner, and the room was thrown into long shadows by the oil lamp. Outside, the promised rain was beginning to tap at the windows. Eustacia leaned back in her chair for a moment, cocking her ear at the sound. She felt the all-too-familiar despair pushing into the front of her mind. Nothing had been accomplished with her defiant older daughter, and now Eustacia had illness to combat as well.

Knuckles banged against the door panels. Wearily Eustacia rose, cloth still in hand, and opened it. Grant, Carla, and Yung Hen stood there, and she could not help a small smile. No matter what, they were loyal friends.

Grant noticed Eustacia had forgotten to put her hat on, but he said nothing. If he could only get beyond that disguise of hers, offer her some real strength and support, even a pair of arms to lean wearily into for a moment.

Carla bustled into the room, pressing her hand down on Collette's forehead. "Oh, dearie, dearie," she clucked. "You know, she was complaining this last week about feeling tired and headachy. And Lord knows, her appetite's fallen off some. She had a nosebleed the other day and an upset stomach. I didn't pay much mind, because you know how kids get things."

"I know, Carla. It's not your fault," Eustacia assured her.

"It's just, Stash, I think she may be real sick. Doctor sick."

"I was just planning to go for Dr. Rhea."

"No, I'll go," Grant put in. "Oh, here, this is part of the reason I came up." He held out a folded piece of paper to Eustacia. The telegraph operator had asked him to deliver it just before he closed.

Mechanically, Eustacia took it, watching Yung Hen slip to Collette's bedside. There was knowledge on his face, and with a sudden sinking sensation, she realized she didn't want to know, but the words came out anyway. "You know what ails her, don't you, Yung Hen?"

"Maybe so. But doctor should say."

The telegram fluttered open between Eustacia's fingers, and then as she glanced down and read it, one of the words squeaked out of her throat: "Typhoid." Eustacia's eyes widened and fastened unbelieving on Collette. The paper shook in her hand. She licked her suddenly dry lips. "It says my father is dead. Peritonitis, and other complications of typhoid fever. Oh, my God! The girls were exposed to typhoid!"

Carla grasped Eustacia's arm, pushing her down into the chair. "Now wait. Maybe that doesn't mean Collette has it."

Eustacia heard Carla's words, but she saw the truth in Yung Hen's eyes.

"I'll get Dr. Rhea on the double," Grant said, and his boots scraped out the door.

Dr. Rhea's examination was done in a hushed room, Eustacia at the foot of Collette's bed, Grant folded into a shadowy corner, Carla slumped in the chair, Yung Hen a swift shadow near the door ready to do the doctor's bidding. For his part, Dr. Rhea noted the rash of pale pink oval spots, the child's slightly distended abdomen, the slowed pulse, and the increasing fever. There was no doubt in his mind that Collette had typhoid fever and was in the second week of it. He looked up and nodded confirmation to the pairs of eyes watching him.

Eustacia's throat constricted. She was afraid with a terrible fear, more awful because it was of something unseen. What she had felt the first time she had driven the stage or when she had fought Arango or been trapped in the Borate mine cave-in was nothing compared to this.

Dr. Rhea was speaking. "I understand Collette's grandfather died of complications of typhoid?"

Eustacia nodded.

"It is safe to say then that both your nieces have been incubating the disease since they left San Bernardino. Each of you may be doing the same right now, from being exposed to them. I should see the other girl."

"I'll go and fetch her, Doc." Carla roused herself up from the chair and headed from the room. The Hurdy-Gurdy House was taking care of itself tonight with a little overseeing from the bartender, Jess.

Eustacia's fingers were biting into the iron foot-rail of the bed. "What can we do? What can we do for Collette?"

"Keep her to herself here first. She'll need near round-the-clock care. It's important at least once a day to wash her back and buttocks and to make sure her mouth is kept clean and rinsed after she eats. Don't be giving her too much food. The current thinking is that it's better to starve the patient a little.

"Now, I can tell you what to expect," Dr. Rhea continued. "There'll be loose bowels. As the fever gets higher, there'll more than likely be mental confusion and delirium. There may be some tremors or even convulsions. These rose spots"—he pointed at Collette's rash—"will fade in four or five days but will leave a brownish stain for a while. By next week, the third week, Collette's tongue will be dry and brown, and the abdominal symptoms will be at their peak. Then, barring complications, the fever will go, and she ought to get better. It's the complications that kill, hemorrhaging from intestinal ulcers, perforation of the bowel where you get the peritonitis." Dr. Rhea straightened. "You got your hands full, Stash. We all do."

"I'll help with the nursing. Don't you fear none." Carla appeared in the doorway next to Yung Hen. Ophelia was not with her.

"Where's the older girl?" Dr. Rhea asked.

Carla threw an agonized look at Eustacia. "She's gone again. She's not in the room Yung Hen gave her."

Eustacia closed her eyes and said nothing. She was numb.

Grant stepped out of his corner. "I'll saddle up and see if I can find her." As he passed Eustacia, he brushed her arm. He saw a tear at the corner of each eye. He could do nothing for her except what he was doing, and so he stepped more quickly.

"Well, I'll see what I can do about heading off an epidemic. I got some medicine down at the store. . . ." Dr. Rhea's words trailed off. Already he was weary, just knowing what was most probably ahead.

"Epidemic?" Eustacia asked softly.

"Yes. You see, the germ is spread from the sick person through excrement, contaminated food, soiled clothing. Water and milk are particularly common agents. A poor sewage system—which Calico has—makes this all easily possible. You'd think they'd learned after the scourge of '83."

It was the same litany Eustacia had heard him recite to Grant—so long ago, it seemed now—when Reynold Whitman had been killed. Eustacia sighed and watched the doctor leave, his shoulders stooped. She moved to Collette's side and began sponging her again. Collette was asleep but restless.

Carla's question broke the stillness. "What about Ophelia?"

Eustacia turned to look at her. Yung Hen had disappeared. "I don't know, Carla. Somehow I just feel like it's been taken out of my hands, that something horrible has begun to grind away at her, and I can't do anything to help her stop it! *Mostly, because she won't let me!*" The tears came then, long and hard and shaking, and the two women stood together in the shadowy room, arms around each other.

At nearly the same moment, Ophelia crouched in the ravine at the mouth of Wall Street Canyon and watched Grant ride out of Calico. It was done, and no one could do anything about it. She had stolen the horse from the lean-to behind the Hurdy-Gurdy and a last round of supplies from Yung Hen's kitchen and had taken them to her father. Now he was safely gone from the deserted mine and on his way back to Arango. He had looked so feverishly excited as he rode away—his cheeks pinked with it. And Ophelia knew where to find him, too, when the time came, for Philip had given her detailed directions to Arango's current camp and had promised to get word to her any time there was a change.

Ophelia straightened up and shook her fist at Grant's dark back. Then she walked into town. She would be glad to fall into bed tonight. Despite the rain, she felt warm and tired—no doubt from the walk and excitement.

By morning there were other typhoid cases. Eustacia and Frank Eberson took the morning stage down to Daggett and back, and by the afternoon run, the known cases had tripled. They returned that evening with an empty stage. Word had reached Daggett, and no one was interested in coming to a typhoid camp. That night, William Curry suspended the line's run indefinitely.

By the second day, Dr. Rhea was running out of medicine. He approached Delameter's freighters, who were putting together a supply run to San Bernardino, and asked them to bring back more. Willingly, they agreed.

Soon after the supply wagons left, there were the first deaths. Collette was not among them, but her disease was progressing exactly as Dr. Rhea had said. Eustacia and Carla took turns bathing her, sitting with her, and laundering the soiled bed linens and night-clothes. Their backs and arms and legs ached from bending over the steaming vat and stirring it.

One afternoon Eustacia walked onto Wall Street for a breath of fresh air. The supply train was due back anytime now, and like many others she glanced anxiously toward the canyon. It was hard, as she looked about her, to believe Calico was the same town. Many of the buildings were draped in black bunting. Eustacia saw Mary Ryan, the only registered nurse in town, come out of one home and enter another. In front of Miller's general merchandising, Mrs. Miller was quietly lining a wooden coffin with black cloth. Some effort at improving the sewage system was being made, and she saw men with shovels farther along the street confronting one of the ditches. The swelling crowds and chatter were gone, the horse traffic almost nonexistent. Even the music drifting out from the saloons and dance halls was subdued.

Suddenly Eustacia realized Grant Whitman was standing beside her. Grant had not been one of the freighters going to San Bernardino. In fact, he no longer worked for Delameter. After Arango's attempted raid on the railroad express car, too many people in the area knew his part in thwarting it and his connection with the army. His cover was no longer viable, and there was no point in trying to preserve it.

As for Grant, he had explained everything to Eustacia, hoping that she would be equally honest with him, but she had stubbornly clung to her disguise. He had not seen much of her, partly because she was usually with Collette and partly because he had been spending most of his time out riding the Mojave trying to learn why Arango had been so quiet of late. He was willing to wager no one else in Calico had given it a thought, they were so preoccupied with the typhoid epidemic.

Dr. Rhea came out of Yung Hen's, saw Eustacia and Grant in the street, and came up to them. "Well, I've just seen Collette. It looks like the fever is much lower. She ought to start getting better now."

"Oh, thank God!" Eustacia burst out, then turned to hurry into the boardinghouse.

Dr. Rhea grasped her arm, "You take a few minutes off. Carla's doing just fine up there." Then a sudden grin split his face, "Hey, look! The freighters are back with the medicine!"

Eustacia and Grant swung toward the canyon. The thick dust cloud belched from it like smoke through a chimney. Then they could hear harness bells and the mule skinners' individualized litanies. Others were

145

streaming into the street now to watch. Curry and Eberson ambled up beside Eustacia and Grant as Dr. Rhea started running toward the train of wagons, shouting, "Mary Ryan! Mary Ryan! Come quick!"

Curry remarked wryly, "I remember when the stage used to get this kind of welcome!"

The entire freight train was in Wall Street now, and Dr. Rhea, flying in front of them, forced them to a halt. He spoke to the first driver, then moved on to the second. Mary Ryan trotted out of the house Eustacia had seen her enter a few minutes before, wiping her hands on her apron. With growing puzzlement, everyone watched the doctor move from one driver to another. Mary Ryan started walking to him.

"Something's wrong," Eustacia whispered.

Grant nodded. Then he and Eustacia were edging toward the freighters with others in the crowd. Eustacia caught a quick glimpse of Dr. Rhea's face dropping momentarily into his hands, and Mary Ryan patting his arm.

Grant sidled up close to the doctor and asked, "What's wrong?"

"The medicine is back in San Bernardino, probably sitting on the loading dock. Every driver thought the other had it."

The doctor looked exhausted, and Eustacia knew it wasn't just the long hours of physical exertion he had been putting in, but the mental strain of trying to save lives—and losing. Her eyes strayed to Miller's general merchandising and the black-lined coffin propped against its wall. She shivered.

Mary Ryan recovered herself first. "We need that medicine." She raised her voice so that it rang loud and clear over the crowd's murmuring. "We need volunteers to ride back to San Bernardino to get the medicine!"

"I'll go!" Eustacia heard herself cry.

Then Grant and Eberson were shouting, "Count us in, too!"

"Take the stage, Stash," Curry ordered. "Damn team needs a good workout, anyway."

Afterward, as Eustacia walked back to Yung Hen's to collect a pack and tell Carla what she was doing, she wondered why she had volunteered. A child of her own was sick and needed care, though Dr. Rhea had just said Collette was recovering. Maybe it was because Eustacia felt responsible for the typhoid epidemic, although there was no guarantee that the bacteria hadn't already been in the camp before Collette and Ophelia's arrival. In any case, she was committed to a grueling one hundred eighty-two mile round trip, knowing there would be more deaths before she returned. She just hoped that Ophelia, Carla, and Yung Hen would not be stricken.

The team was shaking its harness, anxious to be off, when Eustacia walked into Mojave Station. Eberson and Grant were already there, as restless as the horses. In fact, they had helped Harv Miller hitch up.

Eustacia threw her pack on top of the stage roof and then climbed into the box, Grant and Eberson following after her. Both carried shotguns, but she thought better not to remark on it. As she threaded the reins between her fingers, she glanced sideways at the men. "All right, I've figured out why I'm doing this. Why are you two going along?"

Eberson contrived to look shocked. "Since when does a driver get himself no express messenger?"

Grant just grinned. "Because, Stash, you're accident prone."

Eustacia didn't bother to reply. She snapped the whip, and the Calico stage began to bowl down Wall Street.

Coming out of the Calico Mountains, it was a little

warmer at first, but as afternoon encroached, Eustacia discovered the Mojave could be brisk. She was glad for the extra flannel shirt she wore. Grant and Eberson sat hunched forward, as if trying to hold in body heat. Conversation had died off as their muscles began to feel the jolt of the road.

Eustacia pulled the team into a walk. The horses were tiring, and she knew they were going to have to stop for the night. She did not relish the cold hard ground, and she was curious what supplies Curry had loaded inside the coach for them. Idly, she wondered if the slower pace would rejuvenate their conversation, but neither man showed any inclination.

Eustacia glanced sideways at them. Eberson seemed nearly asleep, and looking at him made her own eyes feel itchy and tired. Grant seemed to be staring at nothing in particular. Once again she wondered if he knew her secret. She tried to think back, wondering if she had ever given herself away. There had been so many opportunities for that—the cave-in, Collette's illness. Maybe she just wanted the whole pretense to be over.

Every night, as she had sat with Collette, the thought had come that she was never going to find Philip, that she was on her own. It was ridiculous to think she could drive a stage the rest of her life. To begin with, if and when she was found out, she would no doubt lose the job. Just as important, she did not think she wanted to drive the stage indefinitely; this haul to San Bernardino was just confirming that notion. And her children needed a stable home where their mother was not their uncle.

Feeling the reins in her hands, Eustacia made a decision. When she returned to Calico, she would explore other possibilities of supporting herself and her family, other housing. If prospects were still not good after Collette fully recovered, she would pack them all off back to San Bernardino. Again she glanced at Grant and found herself imagining ways to include him in her future plans.

As for Grant, he had decided that the most numbing part of this journey was having to sit beside Eustacia, trying to figure out how he could get her to discard her disguise. Once he could openly acknowledge who she was, he believed things would go smoothly between them. Even now, they liked each other. Her husband was hardly a consideration any longer, because Grant firmly believed Philip Kibbe was dead. Now it was just this damn disguise that was derailing them.

San Bernardino came and went. If the three had been quiet on the leg down, on the return trip they were downright silent. Curry's team was nearly exhausted, and although it was not strictly regulation, both Grant and Eberson had taken a spell at the reins. Now Eustacia was back driving, and the coach was pounding toward Cajon Pass. The bottles of medicine were packed securely in a compartmentalized wooden box, which was lashed down inside. The stage swept confidently into the pass, and then before Eberson and Grant could even bring up their shotguns, the ride came to an abrupt halt.

There were at least twenty of Arango's men controlling Cajon Pass. Some stood beside the road, rifles pointed at the coach. Others were on outcroppings, their sombreros throwing black, saucerlike shadows. The one mounted man, taller than the others, his face hidden in the shadow of his sombrero, detached himself from the side of the road and rode closer. Eustacia realized it was not Arango, but then came an awful unsureness, and horror spread through her in a hot wave. The bandit stopped beside the driver's box, reached up, and grabbed Eustacia's arm. Grant's shot-gun began to rear, and there were twenty hard clicks as guns were cocked.

"Put it down real easy, boy," Eberson advised Grant softly.

Grant slowly lowered the shotgun, even going so far as to lay it on the floor of the box.

"Eustacia!" Philip doffed his sombrero with his free hand, then dragged his wife off the stage. He dis-mounted and stood beside her. Laughing, he knocked off her hat and turned her out of her bulky jacket.

"What?" Her voice was dead. She looked at her golden-haired husband. There was sweat on his face, and she wondered if he was feverish. "How did you know? What do you want?" It was the same flat tone.

"Ophelia told me, and I want the doctor's medicine. Typhoid has hit Arango's camp. They die like flies. Where is it now?"

"You've seen Ophelia!" Eustacia was incredulous, and then all of Ophelia's little disappearances and ex-cuses made sense.

"Where is it, Eustacia?" Philip staggered a little and wiped the back of his hand across his forehead. "I've got to get back to camp."

"In the coach. Inside," she answered dully. Then suddenly it struck Eustacia what he meant to do, and the black-lined coffin flashed before her eyes. "No, Philip!" She grabbed his arm. "You can't take it! Not all of it! Please listen to me! Your own daughter, Collette, she's sick with typhoid, and Ophelia might be next. Ophelia, Philip! Please—leave us some of it. Please!"

Philip stood still for a minute as though thinking was a great effort. Then he moved slowly toward the coach door, Eustacia trailing him. "All right, then, just some." His words seemed to come more thickly. "But you make sure the girls get all the help they need.

You make sure of Ophelia. She's been such a good daughter."

"I'll make sure." Eustacia could hear the tears in her voice.

Philip gestured to one of the others. The Mexican brought a saddlebag and shouldered Philip and Eustacia out of the way. In the end, the Mexican took more than half of Dr. Rhea's supplies and only stopped when Philip shoved a knee into his back.

The Mexican peeled away then, and as Philip mounted his horse, the men on the outcroppings dropped into the road. A couple of men came riding into the pass, leading a large remuda of horses. In a moment everyone had mounted up, and Philip led the way through the pass and into the vastness of the Mojave.

For a long moment, Eustacia, Grant, and Eberson were frozen. Then, as though weighted with sandbags, Eustacia moved toward the front of the stage. She bent like an old woman and picked up her jacket and hat. She put them on now because she was cold, not because they were a disguise. She was thinking that Philip was sick, probably typhoid. But that would only explain today's irrational actions—not what he had done six months ago.

Grant reached down for Eustacia's hand, helping her up on the box. Balanced on the wheel, she smiled weakly. "You knew about this all the time, didn't you?" She gestured at her masculine attire.

Grant nodded. "I suspected right at the beginning, but I knew that first night when I overheard Carla having her fun teasing you." Afterward, he was glad she did not ask any details of the circumstances.

"Well, I sure as hell didn't know!" Eberson exploded. "Been took in the whole time. Can't believe a woman could handle a rig so good, Stash!"

"Is it all right if I take her into Calico?" Eustacia asked, and Grant nodded.

Eustacia started up the team. She was so tired that she couldn't think of anything else but the leather between her fingers. There would be so many things to think about later.

Grant was silent, his hands folded on his knees. Eustacia's disguise was gone, but Philip Kibbe was alive.

The Calico stage got the welcome it was used to, folks crowding into the street as it stopped at Dr. Rhea's office. In whispered tones, Grant explained to Rhea why his supply was shortened, and the doctor never turned a hair. It was out of his control—and he had no intention of panicking these people.

Slowly, quietly, the stage finally pulled into Mojave Station. William Curry and Harv Miller were waiting, lanterns in hand. "By God!" Eberson slapped his leg. "You got the best driver, and she's a woman! All this time we've been fooled!"

"You *are* a fool," Grant commented bleakly.

Curry threw the lantern light onto all their faces.

"That's right, Mr. Curry." Eustacia lifted her hat.

"My Lord!" Curry exploded.

"Idiot!" Grant bit at Eberson.

"Huh?"

"She could have gone on if you'd kept your mouth shut," Grant added.

Curry looked embarrassed. "You know what this means, Stash. I got to fire you. No man'll ride passenger with a woman driver, once they find out. And they will now." He looked meaningfully at Eberson. "Besides, I know."

"Now y'all hold on!" Eberson said, trying to repair the damage he had done. "I testified to her drivin' when you hired this here Stash, and I'm still testifyin' to it! No call to fire her, 'cept—"

"Except I'm a woman," Eustacia chimed. She clapped the hat on her head. "It's all right, Mr. Curry. I probably wouldn't have done it much longer."

"Sorry, Stash. I really am. Woman or not, you're one of the top drivers I've had," Curry said regretfully. Then he turned away, walking toward the station.

Muttering, Eberson jumped off the box. Dejected, Eustacia and Grant started for the boardinghouse. Their mood was not entirely due to Eustacia's losing her job; more than half of it was the problem Philip Kibbe posed for both of them. No longer was Grant's interest on a personal level. Philip had become part of his job—he would have to hunt him down. As for Eustacia, she was so confused, she did not even know where to begin to unravel her thoughts and feelings. So it was in silence that they walked to Yung Hen's.

Grant came upstairs with Eustacia to see Collette. She looked emaciated and needed to be propped up on pillows, but her face was cool, and she was delighted to have her mother back and to see Grant. Miraculously, he materialized a piece of brown velvet ribbon out of his pocket. Yung Hen sat on the bed, spooning a good clear broth into the little girl.

"Where is Carla, Yung Hen? At the Hurdy-Gurdy?" Eustacia asked.

Yung Hen's eyes were grave as he turned to look at her. "Would she were, Eustacia. She got badly sick four days ago. Typhoid. She is in the next room. I care for her."

Eustacia stripped off her hat and jacket, then quickly washed her hands in the bowl on her dresser. "I'll help, Yung Hen." She planted a kiss on the top of Collette's head and then slipped through the doorway.

Grant caught up to her in the hall, taking her arm.

Eustacia looked up into his face and didn't know what to say. Neither did he. Eustacia covered the moment with her words. "I feel so guilty about Carla. She no doubt caught the typhoid from Collette."

"Not necessarily. It's rampant throughout the camp." Grant had let go of Eustacia's arm and was already moving down the hall away from her. "I've got to go."

Eustacia did not ask him where. Sooner or later, whether tonight or not, it would be after Philip. Quietly, she opened Carla's door. When she finished here, she had to talk to Ophelia.

Next door, Ophelia heard her mother's voice and movements. Laying on her bed in the dim room, she willed her mother's presence away. She felt hot and a little confused, but she had been having the most wonderful golden dream about her father.

Grant did as Eustacia had expected and renewed his search for Philip and Arango, widening his circle daily around Calico into the Mojave Desert. Systematically, he began checking all the small ranches, often riding their acres without the owners knowing. In the evenings, he had taken to having supper with Eustacia. Their conversation flowed back over their lives and the hopes Eustacia had for her children. But it was as though they had tacitly agreed not to mention Philip.

Sometimes Grant sat with Collette, creating small games for her to play. The child was beginning to gain weight again, thanks to the many small meals Yung Hen fixed for her each day. But Grant was barred from Ophelia's room. Eustacia had discovered on the night of her return from San Bernardino that Ophelia also had typhoid fever. Now, whether it was a result of her sickness or an escalation of her dislike for Grant, Ophelia was openly hostile to him. His presence could set off a tantrum the likes of which he had never seen.

During his long rides over the Mojave's barrenness, cold wind on his neck, Grant often pondered his growing relationship with Eustacia. She seemed to enjoy his company. Their backgrounds were certainly similar. Each time they saw each other, Grant thought Eustacia acted a little more accepting, even seeming to need him after all the turmoil and worry she had been through in the last several months. What Grant was not sure of—and he wanted to be—was whether Eustacia depended on him as a friend or as something more. Then there was always the specter of Philip. How was arresting Philip going to make Grant look in Eustacia's eyes?

Eustacia had her hands full nursing both Carla and Ophelia. She couldn't believe it, but she was even more tired than when she had been driving the stage. As she went from task to task, her mind whirled with it. Ophelia's attitude was no consolation, either. Ophelia defended everything her father had done, even his thievery. She accused Eustacia of being disloyal because she delighted in Grant's company. What she accused her mother of doing, Eustacia forcibly put out of her mind—sometimes with a twinge of guilt, because she knew she would like to.

Slowly, Eustacia realized she had to sort out her feelings about Philip before she could make any other decisions—whether about her future plans or Grant. Sixteen years was a long time to be married. There was a lot there—shared joys, shared hard times, births of children. Philip's disappearance had been so wrenching. Then the search had been so long and so fruitless, until that fateful afternoon in Cajon Pass. She was disappointed, so disappointed.

Eustacia could not understand one thing Philip was doing. If she admitted the truth, she felt hurt by that, angry and betrayed. Here the man she thought she had known so well was nothing like he had seemed to her.

At such moments, she thought she had been as blind and foolish as Carla always claimed she was. Everything that Eustacia had always thought dependable, or at least predictable, in her life was crumbling away—except Grant. But now he, too, was a complication, an unknown quantity, until Eustacia could figure out what she had done with the last sixteen years of her life.

So, blinders off—as much as Eustacia cringed doing it—she began to look at her marriage. She started to admit all the little doubts that had accumulated about Philip, certainly not after the first few jobs were lost, but as it became a pattern. Then she remembered all the piecework she had done, new things quickly learned, to salvage the family's financial situation. Eustacia hadn't been helpless or really dependent then. She and the family had survived more often than not because of her. Eustacia saw her self-worth through new eyes.

Yet she was also quick to admit she loved Philip's charm, his quick laugh, his illusion of gallantry, his golden looks. Apparently that was no longer enough for her.

Chapter Ten

Francisco Arango stood in front of the escarpment on Reynold Whitman's ranch, his arms crossed, surveying the litter of bedrolls. Typhoid had struck his camp and was devasting what was left of his small army as effectively as the Gatling guns had the other half. He toed the saddlebag near his feet. It had not been opened yet, but he already knew it did not contain the full supply of medicines. The *compadre* had told him.

Arango glanced at the sweating, swaying American, Philip, and anger gripped him anew. The man was a stinking failure. He could not effectively engineer a raid or do something as simple as bring back a box of medicines. He was useless even as an errand boy.

Arango spit, then swung and struck Philip flat palmed across the face. "Can you not follow simple orders? After you told me about the medicine, I said to bring it to me. I did not tell you to take only part. I did not tell you to let part go into the town. The town has infected my people! Perhaps you yourself are the cause, *gringo!*"

Philip's hand moved across the raised weal on his

cheek. He was having trouble comprehending that Arango had slapped him. He felt as if he were floating above himself and his leader. After failing to bring Arango the mine payroll, he had been grateful for the second chance when his forays into Daggett resulted in news about the medicine. He had brought medicine, relief to the people. He had not failed a third time. Yet Arango was angry and accusing him of incompetence. Perhaps Philip was imagining it all. He had not been feeling well for a week or so now.

Arango, who had not expected a response—who had only tolerated the few he had ever received because he had needed the American—harangued on. "How can I ride with sick men? Soon there will be none at all! It is the silver town's fault, and I will have my vengeance! I will burn the offending thing to the ground. All you *gringos* will pay!"

Arango reached for his revolver, then stilled his hand. He looked at Philip, his eyes flat, hard, and cold. Then, as if he had made some decision, he turned on his heels and walked away.

Philip sighed. Even as naive as he was, he could not miss the significance of the gesture. He had just about completed his usefulness to Arango. Soon he would be dog meat. The sad thing was that Philip could not think what to do about it.

Eustacia sat beside Ophelia's bed, desperately sponging her daughter's fever-wracked body. Ophelia seemed much worse than Collette had been, tossing and screaming out bits and pieces of sentences, her eyes fixed open. Eustacia once again did as Dr. Rhea had instructed and checked the abdominal area. As her fingers gently probed the distended area, Ophelia shrieked, and then that was choked off in a flood of vomit. Eustacia jumped up, grabbed a fresh towel, and swabbed away as much of the foul-smelling stuff as she could. Then, truly frightened, she chucked the towel into a corner and flew out of the room. This time Dr. Rhea had to come!

The violent bout of vomiting seemed to bring Ophelia momentarily around. She realized her mother was not there. What better chance? She needed her father. She had to get to her father. She didn't know why. She was like a desperate, hurt animal, running to find its hole.

Ophelia reeled out of the bed and bounced off a wall. She pulled her nightgown together where her mother had opened it and dragged the blanket from the bed, wrapping it around her. How she got down the hall and stairs and out of the boardinghouse at all was to become anyone's guess, but several people saw her struggle onto a horse and later would tell Eustacia that Ophelia flapped from it like a raggedy flag on a pole. Each of the people who had seen her had been too surprised to react.

Eustacia ran back down Wall Street, ignoring the few shouts from bystanders, and scrambled up the boardinghouse stairs, tripping on her hem and falling once. Dr. Rhea was coming right behind her. She burst into Ophelia's room and abruptly stopped. She was just standing like that, rubbing her skinned elbow, when Grant Whitman came up behind her. He put his hand on top of her shoulder. "She's gone, Eustacia," he said gently. "Some folks saw her take a horse a few minutes ago and ride out of Calico."

"But she is so sick! How could she . . . ? Eustacia stopped the inane question. Ophelia had managed the feat, and it was unimportant how. "She's trying to reach Philip! Of course! She's probably known all along where he is." She took a deep breath and then added, "And where Arango is."

159

"I'll go after her and bring her back," Grant promised. He was silent a moment, looking down into Eustacia's upturned face, then he said the rest of what had to be aired. "This is not just personal anymore, Eustacia. This is not just over a sick girl. This time it's business, too. It's all mixed up together, now."

"Hasn't it always been?"

Grant nodded. Eustacia was right. In the beginning, they had not admitted it. After the medicine was stolen in Cajon Pass, they had avoided speaking of it, hiding in silence. And now Grant could only hope the fear that their relationship might be changed by words had been unfounded. He smiled. "When I get back, we'll talk."

"Of course." Eustacia was very positive.

Grant left then. It did not take him very long to find Ophelia's trail, and at several points he could even make out her distant figure. But he could not catch up. Perhaps her headstart was too good, or his horse slower. Then all of a sudden he knew where she was going. They had just crossed onto Whitman land—land that needed his attention or his release of ownership. Grant felt kind of sick, thought a moment of typhoid, but knew it was because of memories. He wondered if it was fear of those memories that had caused him to overlook that Arango might do the unexpected and return to the escarpment where Reynold Whitman had been murdered. Grant knew he could not ride into the escarpment camp behind Ophelia. He would be killed. So he did the next best thing and rode to a hilly area a little distance away, from where he watched Ophelia ride into Arango's camp.

Disoriented, Ophelia jerked about in the saddle, looking for her father. She vomited again, and the horse reared at the odor. She felt herself falling, and then arms caught her. She looked up into the wavy golden image of her father and thought of candlelight shimmering in a mirror.

Philip was horrified. When Eustacia had told him his daughter was ill, he had selfishly been glad it was Collette. But now it had struck the one he loved best. Ophelia vomited again, and he tried to dab the stuff away with a handkerchief. But there was so much, and it kept coming and coming. Something made Philip glance up, and he saw Arango standing a few feet away, bandanna over his nose and mouth as though he feared Death would enter him through those orifices and take him away, too.

"Ophelia!" Philip croaked. He tightened his grip on her.

So this was what being a father came down to, he thought: holding a dying child and trying to think of something soothing to say. He found himself wildly hoping for a hereafter, forcing himself to believe it existed, to believe he and his princess would never be parted for long. Then he thought he saw fear in Ophelia's eyes, and that hurt as much as her going, as much as a hot knife blade on an open wound. He could not let her suffer that, too.

Philip crooned, "It's all right, baby. We'll be together soon. I know that, and I'll always be there to take care of you."

Confusion whirled in Ophelia's brain. She felt like a drowning person thrashing around for a rope. She could see her father's face, and she fastened on to it. Something irreversible was happening to her, she sensed, something that once again was going to separate her from her father. She could not stand that. A world without him was overwhelming and cold. It felt like falling through a never-ending hole. She could feel the cold already. She was so afraid! His face above her was receding, his beautiful golden face. Then she heard him say he would be coming, too. For now, then, she could bear this.

Ophelia saw only pinpoints of gold. All of a sudden her face exploded with amazement, as though something strong and lethal had attacked from behind. Inside her there was a hot moment of pain, of organs rearranging themselves, shuttling out of the way of a superior force. Then Ophelia Kibbe, at fifteen, was dead of peritonitis.

From the hills, Grant knew the moment, too. He watched Philip double over his child, and he could hear Philip crying on the Mojave wind. Then slowly Grant turned away. All he could think of was that Eustacia had to be told. Perhaps Philip would bring the body into Calico, and perhaps he would not. And then there was the other hurdle that had to be explained and laid to rest between him and Eustacia. If Philip came to Calico, Grant would arrest him.

Grant entered the cool dimness of Yung Hen's boardinghouse and moved silently up the stairs. He found Eustacia in her little room that looked onto the surrounding hills. She had her back to him, and she did not hear him until he had closed the door. In all his life, Grant had not found an easy way to do this, not even with total strangers. He was discovering how much worse it was with someone he loved.

Eustacia turned around. "She made it to Philip, then."

Grant nodded.

"Then I must go to her. Where is the camp?"

"No, Eustacia. Ophelia's dead. She died in your husband's arms."

"Peritonitis. Dr. Rhea said it would most likely be that." Eustacia's voice was dull. She had not moved. Her face was blank of emotion.

Grant looked at her, and he was afraid for her. She was too controlled. This was a crushing blow, and she was not even allowing herself to reel. He fumbled for a gesture, words, anything to help her. He could almost feel the wall between them, and it was more than just Philip. It was as though she was holding every emotion and frustration inside her at bay. He suddenly realized she was terrified to let go, fearing her life and self would fly apart like so much straw thrown into the wind. Instinctively, Grant knew Eustacia could not keep bottling up, or that was exactly what would happen. He also believed that for them ever to have a chance together, she had to confront her grief and her feelings for Philip. They had to do it together, or she would forever hold him away.

Grant knew he had to say something to make her react. "It was quick, Eustacia. Within a few minutes of reaching Philip."

Wonder, then misery, crept into Eustacia's eyes. "She's really dead? Really dead? At fifteen? Where's her body? I need to see her. Why didn't you bring her back?"

"Don't you believe me when I tell you Ophelia's dead?"

"Why should I? Philip's been pulling the wool over my eyes for years." There was an agitated sharpness in Eustacia's voice.

Grant shrugged. He kept his voice even, neutral. "Because I'm not your husband."

"Why didn't you bring her back?" Eustacia demanded again.

Grant deliberately baited her. "If I'd ridden in there, I'd have been shot. Maybe Philip will bring her in." He waited a heartbeat, then added, "Or maybe he'll just scratch out a hole in the sand." It was a cruel thing to say, but he had to pierce through the veneer she had been living behind.

Grant could see Eustacia was fighting for control. Her jaw clenched, her eyes closed, and he imagined she had a vision of sand sifting through blond curls.

"Of course." She was trying to sound reasonable. "It would have been useless for you to be killed." It was Eustacia's last civilized response.

Grant watched her muscles pull her body inward upon itself. He braced himself. He didn't know if she might spring upon him.

"No!" It was a scream of denial of death, high pitched and questioning at the end. Then the word exploded again and again, "No! No! No! No!" It hammered the air like fists, just as her hands were pushing something unseen away from her. "I can't take it! I can't take another thing anymore!"

"Don't take it, then, Eustacia," Grant said softly. He didn't think she heard him. She had begun to cry, but he didn't think she realized that, either. She sat down abruptly on the edge of the bed.

"If Philip doesn't bring Ophelia to me, I'll kill him! I swear I will, after all of this! He's responsible for this whole mess. He runs off and supports some fool, romantic dream. He drags our daughter into it, and she ends up dying. He might as well have killed her himself. Oh, God, what a fool I've been for sixteen years! I've let him lean on me while I picked him up and patched up his world. I've worked so damn hard, and he's never done anything to really help. It's all been superficial. A smile, a word. They're cheap! Actions are valuable! I'm so tired—from the work, the worry, fighting to make ends meet. I'm so tired of pretending. I'm so tired of feeling frustrated at not understanding him!"

Eustacia got up and paced, stumbling against the dresser. She kicked at it, and the water pitcher rocked.

It focused her energy, and she picked it up, deliberately smashing it against the edge of the dresser. She was left with the empty white handle in her hand. "I'm so angry!"

Grant watched something else slip across Eustacia's face—exhaustion. What he feared now was that she just might give up on everything. He came to her, gently pried the pitcher handle out of her fingers, feeling at first resistance, then acquiescence. "All right, you're angry. Are you going to stay that way forever? You have to do something about it. Are you going to tell him?"

"No, it wouldn't make any difference to him. He has no conception of anything but his own needs." Eustacia sighed, resigned.

"Are you willing to go back and accept that situation, Eustacia, trying to live with all you've just said."

Eustacia closed her eyes. She was feeling calmer now, as if screaming and crying had temporarily resolved some great pressure she had carried for so long. Grant was asking her the same questions she had been asking herself in a roundabout way when she thought Philip was dead. Suddenly she realized that in a strange way he really was. He would never seem the same to her. The truth was too bright. What were her actual feelings now? She searched past the hysteria, past the anger and disgust, and found nothing. Then she realized that her anger and disgust merely kept Philip's image alive, specterlike, allowing him to always transpose himself between her and anything she wanted. She deserved more than that. She was worth more than that.

Eustacia opened her eyes and looked at Grant. His concern was obvious in the creases on his forehead, in the almost hurt tentativeness in his eyes. "No, I will never go back," Eustacia answered.

There was rapid rapping on the door panels, and

then, totally uncharacteristically, Yung Hen burst in. He looked in much pain. "A rider comes, Eustacia. He brings Ophelia."

Eustacia and Grant followed Yung Hen into the hallway and down to a window facing the street. Eustacia did not know what would happen when she looked. Then she had to. She saw Philip sitting in the saddle, Ophelia cradled in front of him. She waited for the anger. Nothing. And she realized with the vanishing of anger had also gone the love.

Sighing, Eustacia turned away. "It's almost as if I knew all along I was going to lose Ophelia. She's been slipping away bit by bit ever since Philip disappeared. Almost daily I've been dealing with that loss."

Eustacia began walking back up the hall. She had just realized something else, as well. Ophelia had been the glue that had held Eustacia to Philip for a good many years now. If she had wanted to keep her daughter, then Philip also had to be accepted. Now Ophelia was gone, and there no longer was anything to bind Eustacia to Philip.

Slowly, Grant followed Eustacia. "I have to arrest him. I'll be back to talk about it, if you'll see me."

"I don't care about him anymore. I don't care what happens to him anymore. Come back—and, Grant, thank you."

As he walked out of the boardinghouse, Grant felt he had never walked more slowly or with more lead in his boots. Eustacia had come the full path, but what lay ahead? For him, right now, it was Philip. Grant had doubtful jurisdiction in arresting Philip, but the Calico sheriff certainly had the power, since Philip had robbed the Run Over Mine and Mill payroll. Just to be safe, Grant made a citizen's arrest.

Dr. Rhea was standing nearby, directing the lowering of Ophelia's body into waiting arms. "She best go to

Yung Hen's for the lying-in." Speculatively, he sized up Philip. The man was sweaty and gray, his face loose and soft like runny putty. When Dr. Rhea heard Grant make his arrest—an action he was sure Philip Kibbe did not really hear or understand—he edged closer. "There's no point taking him to the jail, Grant. He's too sick with typhoid. Best take him to the boardinghouse, too, and I'll be along to see what's to be done."

Grant nodded his agreement, and with his arm around Philip's waist, he half walked, half dragged him along the boardwalk and finally up Yung Hen's stairs. Eustacia met them at the top landing and, pointing to an open door, said, "In there, please."

Grant dropped Philip on top of the mattress, pulled off his boots, then helped Eustacia roll him under the quilt. He felt on unsure ground, and so to cover his unease, he remarked, "Dr. Rhea said he's coming." Then Grant found himself backing out of the room. He would give Eustacia a little time and space.

When Grant's footsteps had died away, Eustacia turned and looked down at Philip. She stared with curiosity at this new person she saw. She felt totally neutral, and she knew that Grant had given her a great gift in bringing her through her feelings.

Even to Eustacia's untrained eye, Philip was clearly dying. There would be no need to tell him she was leaving him, and she was relieved at that. It was one less unpleasantness to experience.

Philip's eyes flickered open, red rimmed, the blue seemingly faded. "Eustacia," he sighed. "Ophelia, our daughter, she's dead." He started to sob. The rest of the sad story came through heaving gulps. "In my arms. She was so sick. I am so sorry, Eustacia. I was tricked by Arango's fine words, but now I've discovered he's a monster. He persecutes me even though I gave up my family—only temporarily, my dear, because I was always coming back—and he was disgusted and afraid for himself when Ophelia died. I will turn my gun on him. I swear it. And afterward, Eustacia, my darling, I will make everything up. I can do it. Make it as before. And Collette, my little elfin, there is nothing I won't shower on her. We'll be one happy family again. You'll see. I can do it. Eustacia, do you believe me? You'll give me my chance?"

"Yes, Philip, I believe you mean what you say."

Eustacia felt no guilt. She noticed darkness was falling, and she lit the kerosene lamp and twitched the curtains closed. By then, Dr. Rhea had arrived. She waited through his visit, then did what she could to make Philip comfortable. When he had fallen into a restless sleep, she slipped into the hall. Grant stood across from her in the shadows, back against the wall, arms folded across his chest, head bent forward. His whole posture told her he was tired. The look he fastened on her told her he needed to know where he stood.

Eustacia went to him and leaned her head against his shoulder. "Philip is dying, Grant. Dr. Rhea barely gives him a day. He thinks that he is hemorrhaging from an ulcerated intestine. So, Grant, I didn't bother to tell him I was leaving him, that I had made my choice and it is you."

Grant's arms unfolded and snatched her into them. "Oh, I was hoping, Eustacia. I thought so, but I couldn't be sure."

"Be sure," Eustacia said as she reached up and pulled Grant's head down. They were both ready for their kiss.

Out on the Mojave, Arango's eyes blazed with the glow of the firelight. He sat cross-legged, huddled forward, and he was furious. A *compadre* had informed him

Philip was nowhere to be found in the camp. Others had sworn that he had taken a horse and left with the dead girl in the direction of Calico. Arango had expected him to bury the girl in the desert, but this did not seem to be. No doubt Philip was a traitor, gone to warn the silver camp of Arango's plan to level it. But that would not be enough. Even as Philip uttered his warning, Arango would be upon him and the town, wasting it.

Snapping a stick, Arango leaped to his feet, shouting in Spanish. His will would be done.

Chapter Eleven

Carla opened her door a crack and listened to Grant and Eustacia in the dim boardinghouse hallway. Slowly she was recuperating from her own bout with typhoid. Today she had been able to cross her room twice. She wasn't used to her haggard appearance yet or the way her flesh hung from sudden weight loss, but these things would be remedied with time. Curiosity at the soft voices led her to open her door, and she overheard part of Eustacia's conversation and witnessed her and Grant's embrace. As soon as Carla was sure they were gone, she slipped from her room and approached the door behind which Philip Kibbe lay. Carla wanted to see the man Eustacia had sought so desperately and who had disappointed her so greatly.

Quietly, Carla let herself in. The room was only slightly lighter than the hall, prismed with shadows. She could hear the ragged breathing from the bed, and she crept nearer, grasping one of the four posts for support. She looked down, and suddenly her legs felt like they were made of running water. "Emil!" she gasped. In that awful moment, everything came clear to

Carla, the worst part being that she had been having an affair with Eustacia's husband. She told herself that Eustacia must never know. She was facing enough problems without having to deal with that sordid knowledge.

Gently, a hand dropped on Carla's shoulder. She jerked, her neck twisting to see who stood behind her. Then, in a hoarse whisper, she said, "Dammit, Yung Hen! You trying to give me heart failure?"

"You know the truth now, isn't it so?"

"Yes."

"You do not look good. Come back to your room. It is nearly over for him, and the whole thing will fade from your memory."

"With a little help it will. Yung Hen, go get my laudanum." When she saw his disapproving look, Carla said in a stronger voice, "Just go do it, Yung Hen! No lectures now, please."

He nodded, and Carla allowed herself to be led back to her room. When she was alone, she stared in the mirror over the dresser. Her face was ashen. She felt used and tricked like she never had before. True, she had realized that things were crumbling between her and Emil—Philip. But she had not expected them to shatter like broken glass. The guilt she felt about Eustacia was the worst. All the time Eustacia had been hopelessly searching, Carla had had Philip in her embrace. She felt cheap, and even in her worst days of whoring she had never felt that way. Whoring had been something to do for survival.

Yung Hen tapped at the door and handed Carla a small brown bottle. She took it and shooed him away. She did not miss the long look he gave her; she chose to ignore it.

Carla slumped down on the bed. It hardly seemed worth the effort to go on. Just when a body got going good, something happened to slap her down. Why should she go on at all? Carla wondered. The Hurdy-Gurdy House wasn't that much to go back to. Eustacia and Grant would, no doubt, go someplace else to start new lives. She would be alone again with just Yung Hen to depend on. Sooner or later, Calico would play out, and she felt too old to move on. She would be just one more living ghost in buildings that creaked conversation with the desert wind.

To hell with it then, Carla was thinking. She uncorked the laudanum, intending on a good pull, a whole bottle worth of pull. Then the thought flashed through her mind that she was a damn fool. She didn't credit herself enough. Carla had survived, however unevenly, in circumstances that would have bowled most people over. She thumped the little cork back into the neck of the bottle. Carla had not overcome typhoid to throw it all away over a man, especially a man the likes of Philip Kibbe. Moreover, she was going to salvage something out of this mess—for Eustacia's sake, if nothing else. Carla was going to impress on Philip that there need not be any deathbed confessions just to relieve his own sick soul.

Carla let the laudanum bottle slip to the floor and lay back on the bed, twitching the comforter over her. She was tired from her weakness. She would rest until the boardinghouse grew silent, and then she would once more visit Philip's room.

When Carla awoke, pale gray light filled her room. The laudanum bottle had been picked up off the floor and now sat on the dresser—Yung Hen's doing, no doubt. Carla cracked a smile. Then she sat bolt upright, afraid that she might be too late to get to Philip. Anxiously pushing off the comforter, Carla swung her feet to the floor. She listened for other sounds, but the boardinghouse seemed asleep. Carla left her room and hurried down the hall to Philip.

Inside, his ragged breathing was less regular. Carla went and stood over the bed. There was already the faint smell of death emanating from Philip. She called his name.

Philip's eyes slitted open. He saw a shape above him but could not tell who it was, except it seemed more feminine than masculine. He guessed Arango hadn't got him yet.

"Philip! Do you know me? It's Carla. I gotta talk to you!"

This person seemed determined on talking to him, and Philip wondered why. He was also trying to remember where he was.

"Listen, Philip," the voice was going on. "You're not long for it. I'll give you that honest enough."

Philip wondered who the woman was who called herself Carla.

"Listen, Philip, for Eustacia's sake you've got to keep silent about us and all the horrible things you've been part of. You've got to let her go clean from Calico. She's got a whole new life in front of her. You don't need to muddy it up with bad memories. Confession ain't going to make a damn bit of difference. For me, either, when my time comes. You see, you and I are cut from the same cloth—both dreamers, fooled by illusions, and because we are so blind, swimmers in the gutter."

Philip was thinking he did not know how to swim. An image was forming in his hot head of a woman's horrified expression and blowing feathers and lots of blood. Then he remembered Carla and the killing of her chickens, and that made him think about Arango again—and Calico. The town name tinkled like a distant bell. Suddenly he remembered he had something urgent to tell.

Philip tried to sit up. He tried to find saliva in his mouth. When Carla saw his lips working, she grabbed a cup of water from the rickety nightstand and helped him drink. Now with enough moisture in his mouth to form words, he croaked, "Arango is coming here. Level Calico. Revenge for the typhoid. May be coming even now. Warn! Warn!" Then Philip fell back.

Transfixed, Carla stood rooted beside the bed. Who could she tell? Then she thought of Grant. He was army—he would know what to do.

Carla burst into the hallway calling for Grant. When he did not appear from one of the rooms, she flew downstairs, both hands gripping the banister, fighting lightheadedness. He did not answer her cries downstairs, either. The early Chinese laying out place settings stared at her in surprise, and also the ones in the kitchen as she looked for Yung Hen, hoping he would know where Grant was and would go for him. Yung Hen was not there, and she could not make herself understood to the others—either about Yung Hen or Grant. They laughed and made signs about fevers and heads.

Panicky, Carla burst out of the kitchen into the alley between the boardinghouse and the Hurdy-Gurdy. She ran directly into Francisco Arango.

It seemed all of the cool morning flooded into Carla's lungs. She tried to back away, but he held fast to one arm. She drew herself up and demanded, "What do you want? Certainly not Philip! He is as good as bones right now!"

"Then you are right. I certainly do not want him, but I think he has told you my men wait only half a mile up Wall Street Canyon. I think he has told you I mean to raze Calico, and if he has not, then I have just told you, and the situation is still the same."

"A pox on you, Francisco Arango!" Carla bit out viciously.

Arango's eyes narrowed, as hard and bright as black agates. "You were about to warn someone. Is it that Grant Whitman? Well, now you never will, *mi amiga!*"

Carla saw the blow coming and tried to bend out of its way. Arango's fist crashed into the side of her face, shattering the cheekbone, the pain so fierce her whole being seemed set upon by hundreds of small licking fires. That was when she knew he meant to beat her to death. She had no strength left for that kind of punishment.

Carla was so far flung to one side that it was easy to grope under her clothes for the knife held in her garter. Her fingers pinched around the hilt, pulled it free, and swung it up. The blade sliced through material, hampering the force of her blow, but she drove the blade into Arango's chest. The wound was high and not mortal. She pulled the knife free, meaning to strike again, but Arango was ready, and he twisted her wrist until the knife fell from her hand. Carla raked his face, but Arango kicked her in the stomach and she fell. She did not see him snatch up her knife. Then he was straddling her, and she saw the flash of it plunging toward her.

"*No!*" Carla's shriek turned into a scream, shrill and agonized, which echoed like crashing waves as the knife slashed and cut again and again. In the stunned silence that followed, Arango ran.

Eustacia was the first one in the alley, responding to Carla's hideous screams only seconds behind Arango's departure. She dropped beside the shredded bundle of bubbling red cloth. Carla's chest was spurting blood, and there was a pink froth on her lips.

"Arango did it," Carla whispered. "Going to level

175

Calico. Men half mile up canyon." She started coughing, and great clots were flung on Eustacia.

"Dear God in heaven," Eustacia prayed. She skirted around and pulled Carla's shoulders into her lap.

There were bubbling sounds, despite Eustacia's effort to elevate Carla, and Eustacia figured Carla was drowning in her own blood. She knew it was hopeless, the end only a few minutes away. Motherlike she stroked back hair from Carla's foam-flecked face and asserted, "They ought to name the whole town after you, Carla, after what you've just done."

Carla's frightened, pain-filled eyes fastened on Eustacia. "Been my friend," she gurgled. Then it fell to a mutter, much like a stream drying up over pebbles. "Just a damn shame to survive men, suicides, and typhoid to still die in an alley like a whore."

"Oh, no, Carla! Not you! You've always been anything but!"

Carla never heard Eustacia. She was silent. Even her bleeding had slowed to a trickle.

Eustacia looked down into the quiet, pale face and tried to see the bawdy woman who had pulled her off the street and into the Hurdy-Gurdy. She tried to see the indignation that had played across her features during Yung Hen's near hanging, the lopsided smile of self-deprecation. She could find none of it. It was all gone with the woman's soul.

Tears were silently coursing down Eustacia's face as she slipped Carla's head off her lap. There was Carla's warning to give the camp, her last act of courage that had cost her so dearly.

As she was standing, Eustacia heard a commotion on Wall Street, shouts of fire. A man near the mouth of the alley pointed upward. Automatically Eustacia followed his gesture, her eyes scanning Yung Hen's roof. Then from beyond she saw flames shoot over the roofline.

The fire was atop the Globe Restaurant. Simultaneously, she thought she heard Grant's voice shouting for help from the street.

Indecision gripped Eustacia. If the fire spread, the boardinghouse was in danger, and Collette and an incapacitated Philip were inside. Yet Grant had called for aid. Eustacia watched the fire a moment more, wondering if a spark from the restaurant's kitchen had started it or if it were part of Arango's handiwork. Then, as a whirling flume of sparks burst like fireworks into the morning grayness, Eustacia ran for the back door of the boardinghouse, colliding with Yung Hen.

"What happened, Eustacia? I was in the cellar, and the boys in kitchen say they heard terrible sounds out here in the alley."

Mute for a moment, Eustacia gestured behind her. Then she found her voice. It was cloggy sounding with tears and phlegm. "Arango has killed Carla."

Yung Hen did not move a muscle. His gaze shifted behind her.

Eustacia hurried around him then, shouting, "There's also fire on the Globe roof!" Then she was racing through the kitchen and upstairs, calling for Collette.

A few late-rising boarders were milling in the hallway. One, hearing Eustacia call Collette, said he had seen her go downstairs a few minutes before. That just left Philip to get out, then. If Collette wasn't in the dining room or parlor, which Eustacia could check on her way out, she was probably already outside.

Philip was in a near stupor when Eustacia reached him. Somehow, with bullying slaps and shouts and determination, she got him on his feet. Then, with him leaning heavily on her, they started out of Yung Hen's.

Grant had been returning to the boardinghouse when Arango sprang from the alley. Grant drew his gun and shouted as Arango skidded to a halt close to the boardinghouse doorway. At the same instant, Collette burst through it. Like a striking snake, Arango's arm flashed out and caught the little girl around the neck. He pulled her backward against him and drew his own revolver.

Under his breath, Grant swore. The people in the street, who had rushed outside to look at the fire, heard the commotion and turned toward Arango and the girl. Arango, dragging Collette with him, backed off the boardwalk and into the street. When his attention was caught by a burst of sparks and a pop as two other buildings caught, the crowd began to edge toward him, but he flashed a vicious look at it, malevolently shaking his head.

Eustacia cleared the boardinghouse doorway with Philip into a world of smoke and heat and a subdued yellow light as flames lit the gray morning. Everyone's attention seemed directed at something else besides the fire. Then she saw her daughter and Arango, and she screamed, *"Collette!"*

Eustacia's shriek riveted Arango's attention on her and, more importantly, on Philip. Philip shook off his stupor, saw the Mexican gripping his daughter, and broke from Eustacia's hold, enraged. He grabbed a pistol from an onlooker. Arango, having trouble aiming his revolver and controlling the squirming child, flung her from him, firing even as Philip did. Grant and the others, caught in the crossfire, dropped to the boardwalk and street.

Suddenly, Grant saw Arango fall. Then Philip collapsed. Grant scuttled to Arango and saw that he was dead, but could find no bullet holes. Puzzled, Grant turned him over. Embedded between Arango's shoulderblades was a Chinese meat cleaver. Slowly, Grant raised his eyes and met Yung Hen's stoic expression.

Collette still lay in the street, curled in a half-fetal position, her body shaking with sobs. Nodding at Yung Hen, Grant walked away from the Mexican bandit, picked up Collette, and carried her back to Eustacia. Eustacia sat on the boardwalk in front of the boarding-house, unaware the roof was ablaze, Philip's head cradled in her lap on Carla's dried blood.

Grant set Collette next to her mother, and the little girl curled into her arm and cried into her shoulder. A cursory look told Grant that Philip had not been shot either. He moved behind Eustacia, staring ahead at buildings across the street that were catching from flying sparks.

Philip's eyes were glazing with the film of death. He swallowed hard. He felt so hot and funny, but he could still make out Eustacia. He had to reaffirm. "I finally did something right, Eustacia, didn't I? I killed an evil man and rescued our daughter. You see, things are going to be all right for us now, just like I said before, aren't they?"

Eustacia had tears in her eyes for Philip and his world of illusions, ironically stable and intact to the end. Then she thought that it did not matter. If it made things easier for him—now of all times—it was a blessing. She found the words. "Yes, Philip, of course."

Philip smiled, golden and seraphimlike. In the next minute, he was dead, and the smile was still on his face.

"Come on." Grant was touching Eustacia's shoulder. "We've got to move. The building's burning, along with most of Calico." He moved around Eustacia and slung Philip up over his shoulder, laying him gently in the middle of the street.

With Collette in her arms, Eustacia followed. Someone had dragged Arango from the area of the burning buildings. Farther off, she saw Carla's body, Yung Hen squatting next to it in grief. The Hurdy-Gurdy House was burning now, and just then Jess, the bartender, came dashing out the front door, Carla's ornate hurdy-gurdy organ cradled in his arms. The air was filled with a great deal of swirling ash, and it looked like the entire town might go. People were hurrying out of businesses and homes with assorted belongings.

Then suddenly Eustacia remembered what Carla had said about Arango. "Grant."

He looked down at her.

"Carla told me that Arango's men are half a mile up Wall Street Canyon. Do you suppose they'll come in without their leader? A fire provides a lot of confusion. Maybe it was even the signal."

"Good thought, Eustacia. We'll send Arango's body out. That should make the rest think twice, knowing he's dead."

Grant signaled to some of the other men. They loaded Arango's body across a horse, lashed it down, led it to the mouth of Wall Street Canyon, and slapped it on its way on the road out of Calico.

As Grant was walking back up Wall Street to Eustacia, he heard Joe Miller, the owner of the general merchandising, declaring to other businessmen, "When we get the town back up, for every three or four wood buildings we ought to have one of adobe. A firebreak, kind of." There was muttered agreement.

By the time Grant reached Eustacia, she had Collette quieted and standing solemnly beside her. "Look," Eustacia breathed, pointing toward Mojave Station. Frank Eberson, Harv Miller, and William Curry were pulling the stage and team clear of the buildings that had just begun to smolder. With a few seconds to spare, Mojave Station popped into pockets of flames that fed hungrily toward each other.

Collette shivered a little, her palm sweaty in

Eustacia's hand. "Mama, what are we going to do now?"

Squeezing Collette's hand, Eustacia declared, "We are going to be happy. We are going to be a family." She linked her arm through Grant's.

"Come on, Collette," Grant said, swinging her up on his shoulders. "You'll have a better view from here. We're going to rebuild Calico."

Epilogue

While the ashes were barely cool that September of 1887, Calico's residents began reconstruction. The businessmen agreed with Joe Miller, and every third or fourth building was adobe, serving as a firebreak. The first adobe house was built from materials hauled from a nearby dry lake. Subsequently, however, the residents discovered the hard red clay of Calico itself was superior, and so deep basements were dug and the removed clay mixed with water and formed into walls. Though roofless today, these walls and gaping basements can still be seen in the now-deserted town.

During the years of the silver boom, the people of Calico saw more than their share of excitement, from the near-lynching of a Chinese man to a fatal mine explosion in nearby Borate. The payroll of the Run Over Mine and Mill was indeed stolen, though the money was never recovered, with suspicion lingering that the funds disappeared into the ranks of the posse. The real robber was caught, however, and was killed in self defense by one of the posse members.

Dorsey the mail dog's fate was much happier. When

James Stacy sold his mining interest in Calico, he gave the dog to a dear friend and rich lumberman in San Francisco, with whom Dorsey lived out his life.

After surviving fire and a typhoid epidemic, during which the desperately needed medicine was indeed left behind by freighters, Calico eventually emptied out, almost to be forgotten, when the silver mines played out. But around 1957, Walter Knott of Knott's Berry Farm in Los Angeles, California, bought the seventy-five-mile tract that includes the Calico townsite. He had extensive plans for restoring it, beginning with clearing away debris and reinforcing old buildings. Knott's interest came from growing up on a Mojave homestead and working in the Calico mines in the summer of 1910. It is with thanks to him that something of Calico lives on today for all to see.

★ WAGONS WEST ★

A series of unforgettable books that trace the lives of a dauntless band of pioneering men, women, and children as they brave the hazards of an untamed land in their trek across America. This legendary caravan of people forge a new link in the wilderness. They are Americans from the North and the South, alongside immigrants, Blacks, and Indians, who wage fierce daily battles for survival on this uncompromising journey—each to their private destinies as they fulfill their greatest dreams.

☐	24408	**INDEPENDENCE!**	$3.95
☐	24651	**NEBRASKA!**	$3.95
☐	24229	**WYOMING!**	$3.95
☐	24088	**OREGON!**	$3.95
☐	24848	**TEXAS!**	$3.95
☐	24655	**CALIFORNIA!**	$3.95
☐	24694	**COLORADO!**	$3.95
☐	20174	**NEVADA!**	$3.50
☐	25010	**WASHINGTON!**	$3.95
☐	22925	**MONTANA!**	$3.95
☐	23572	**DAKOTA!**	$3.95
☐	23921	**UTAH!**	$3.95
☐	24256	**IDAHO!**	$3.95

Prices and availability subject to change without notice.

Buy them at your local bookstore or use this handy coupon: